up the Bozeman Pass.

Now he worried that if he followed the well-beaten trail he'd again run into the posse. Then again, he worried he wouldn't, as they had his weapons and his money. He planned to get back his brand-new Winchester Model 73, his well-worn Remington revolver, and his money. He'd also lost a bandolier of ammunition, .44-caliber shells that fit both weapons. He'd stripped that bandolier off a Piegan brave who'd had intentions of relieving him of his scalp but got sent to the happy hunting ground instead . . . thanks to the old converted Army Remington.

All his things had some sentimental value. He laughed to himself at the thought as Blue plodded along. He wondered if taking an Indian's life was actually something to impart "sentimental value," then decided saving his own was sure as hell sentimental to him. He'd made friends with a number of Indians while in the prairie, but there were renegade bands about. Since Crazy Horse had surrendered, these fragmented groups, usually made up of young hotheads, seemed to be even more hostile than usual.

It had been most of a decade since he'd seen his brother, Liam. Liam was most of two years older, had left St. Louis at sixteen, two years before Sam reached that age and followed suit. And even though he'd tried, Sam had never caught up with his brother. Their pa had been a river man, and both the boys and their ma considered it an unfit life. Even at that, Sam would have stayed with their ma but the consumption took her to her reward, and while the old man was downriver, Sam had lit a shuck.

He was looking forward to seeing Liam.

It was midafternoon when he heard the distant sound of hoofbeats. He reined a hundred yards up off the trail into a deep cut where, as he peered over, his head just cleared the wall, and he watched to see who was in such a hurry.

Sure as hell's hot it was the same bunch who'd rousted him out of a good night's sleep and relieved him of his things.

Well, he decided he'd use this to his advantage. The pursued became the pursuer. They were riding much too fast to be doing any kind of tracking, and as he suspected they passed where he'd reined off the trail without noticing the sign. He waited until the hoofbeats faded from earshot, then rode back up on the trail and followed at a smooth canter. He'd have to

Stranahan

L. J. Martin

Thorndike Press • Waterville, Maine

Published in 2005 by arrangement with Pinnacle Books, an imprint of Kensington Publishing Corp.

Thorndike Press® Large Print Western.

The tree indicium is a trademark of Thorndike Press.

The text of this Large Print edition is unabridged.
Other aspects of the book may vary from the original edition.

Set in 16 pt. Plantin by Carleen Stearns.

Printed in the United States on permanent paper.

Library of Congress Cataloging-in-Publication Data

Martin, Larry Jay.
    Stranahan / by L. J. Martin.
       p. cm. — (Thorndike Press large print Westerns.)
    ISBN 0-7862-7611-8 (lg. print : hc : alk. paper)
       1. Montana — Fiction.   2. False testimony —
Fiction.   3. Fugitives from justice — Fiction.   4. Large
type books.   I. Title.   II. Thorndike Press large print
Western series.
PS3563.A72487S77 2005
813′.54—dc22   2005003438

Stranahan

As the Founder/CEO of NAVH, the only national health agency solely devoted to those who, although not totally blind, have an eye disease which could lead to serious visual impairment, I am pleased to recognize Thorndike Press* as one of the leading publishers in the large print field.

Founded in 1954 in San Francisco to prepare large print textbooks for partially seeing children, NAVH became the pioneer and standard setting agency in the preparation of large type.

Today, those publishers who meet our standards carry the prestigious "Seal of Approval" indicating high quality large print. We are delighted that Thorndike Press is one of the publishers whose titles meet these standards. We are also pleased to recognize the significant contribution Thorndike Press is making in this important and growing field.

Lorraine H. Marchi, L.H.D.
Founder/CEO
NAVH

* Thorndike Press encompasses the following imprints: Thorndike, Wheeler, Walker and Large Print Press.

One

To say that being awakened with the cold ring of a muzzle pressed between your eyes rattles your backbone would be like saying the sun rises in the east.

Sam Stranahan was no tenderfoot, having trapped furs and hunted buffalo, been a herdsman and occasionally a freighter, and even panned a little color now and then. And all this before he had thirty years, which were behind him as of yesterday, if he had his days right.

He was no stranger to guns, but this was a first for him.

He lay flat on his back on his bedroll, his saddle for a pillow, the morning sun just cutting the horizon and somewhat blinding him.

"Is there something I can do for you fellas?" he asked, afraid to flinch, afraid to raise a hand to shield his eyes from the sun. His breath roiled in the morning cold.

"You were in Bozeman yesterday?" The question came from the gravelly voice behind the cold steel resting between Sam's eyes.

He couldn't bring himself to move his head to see, but he sensed there were more men present than the three he could make out beyond the occluding gun hand.

"I was not," he offered quietly. "I've been dodging redskins for the last week, coming up the Yellowstone. I figured I'd be in Bozeman tomorrow sometime."

"Track said you come into this camp from the southwest."

"I backtracked to the river late yesterday, wantin' to camp by water. . . . I was startin' to whiff myself."

The man with the gun cackled.

Sam was beginning to feel the heat rise in his backbone, having to explain his personal ablutions to a bunch of strangers. Still, he kept his voice low and constant. "You're getting my hackles up, mister. Take your damned weapon off'n my forehead."

"Or what?"

Sam could sense some humor in the man's voice. It was clear the man accosting him thought he had nothing to fear.

"Do as he says, Rusty," another voice

8

rang out. This one seemed to have some authority behind it.

"I ain't convinced," the voice behind the cold muzzle said. The man referred to as Rusty turned to glance at the voice of authority.

Sam slapped the gun away with his right hand, catching the man's wrist with his left and backhanding him hard across the mouth as the right came back.

Although he knocked that one momentarily senseless, the rain of blows and kicks that fell upon him made him curl up in a fetal position, before getting his legs under him. As he drove up to his feet, he caught the flash of a descending rifle barrel out of the corner of his eye, and heard the crack of iron on bone before everything went black and whirlpooled as he slumped back to the cold ground.

"Thacker, what do you think?"

The man speaking was a ruddy-complexioned redhead with hatchet features, his hat now on the ground six feet away. He backhanded a trickle of blood from the corner of his mouth, a result of the blow from the now unconscious man on the ground.

Thacker wore a star on his vest, a vest encircling a barrel of a torso. His head was a keg atop no neck set on wide shoulders, with a hat large enough that it had to have been custom made. He pulled a gold pocket watch from his vest pocket by its gold chain and checked the time before he ordered, "Search his bedroll and pack. I'd guess he'd be who he says, as he's only one and we been trackin' three, but it's worth a gander."

There were six of them. They'd come into Sam Stranahan's cottonwood-protected camp just before sunup. Two of them, Cree Indians, had moved Stranahan's weapons out of reach before the redhead had shoved the muzzle between his eyes.

They were a posse from Bozeman, who'd come downriver in pursuit of a gang of stage robbers — robbers who, as a result of their last of many holdups, were also murderers, as they'd shot the man riding shotgun dead center in the chest. The shotgun guard was the redhead's brother.

That they were tired and impatient was an understatement. All of them were dusted from head to boot, and sweat had trailed down their cheeks and foamed the withers and muddied the flanks of their mounts, even in the morning chill. They'd been riding hard, all night, only pausing at the Big Timber stage stop for a quick breakfast of beans, fried eggs, and side pork. Even the two Cree trackers were tired and eager to get back to their women.

As three of the white men, including the redhead, ruffled though the bedroll and pack, Stranahan began to regain consciousness.

Just as he sat up, rubbing the goose egg on his forehead, the redhead held up a money belt triumphantly. "By all that's holy, this is the son of a bitch what shot Howard."

Thacker still sat quietly astride his tall gray Tennessee Walker. "Pacovsky, it ain't no sin for a man to have a little money."

Something about the tone of their voices and their attitude told Sam they knew he wasn't the man they sought. Then why were they harassing him? Unless they wanted his rig and whatever else he had.

The redhead called Pacovsky thumbed through the wad in the money belt. "A little, hell. There's ten thousand here at least. Some gold coin and a hell of a bunch of scrip."

Sam tried to get to his feet, but one of the other men shoved him back to his butt. Sam spat blood, backhanding his mouth again, then managed, "There's just a little over thirty-eight hundred of my hard-earned there in scrip and coin, but it don't surprise me that this brindle-topped fool can't cipher."

The redhead took a step forward, but Sam spun and got his legs between them, threatening a kick, and the man held up.

"Let him stand," Thacker said.

Sam pulled on his boots, then slowly climbed to his feet.

Thacker eyed him. "You're ever bit of six feet. Hair color's black and down to your shoulders, and the blue eyes seem right. You got a name?"

"Stranahan, not that it's any of your by-God bloody business."

"More Irish trash," the sheriff mumbled. The man with the badge seemed to be making up his mind; then he motioned to the one he'd called Pacovsky. "Bring me the money, then shackle him in the saddle."

"The hell you will," Stranahan spat.

Thacker slipped a scattergun from a scabbard alongside the gray with the whisper of cold steel on leather, leveled it on Stranahan's midsection, then ratcheted back the hammers. He growled, "Son, we can do this my way, or your way, but it seems your way is the bloody way. This ol' ten gauge is loaded with cut-up box nails.

12

Do you want a taste? If you do, the last thing you see'll be your guts on those rocks behind you. Or do you want to come along easy-like and see what the judge has to say?"

"I didn't do nothing to give you call —"

"Judge Talbot will sort it out."

Rusty Pacovsky gave him a boot to the backside, and Stranahan stumbled forward, in the direction of his horse. "Git over to that ugly grulla, and we'll shackle you after you're mounted."

Sam Stranahan thought again about how pleasing it had been to slap this redheaded fool, and would be to do so again, but the scattergun still lay trained on his midsection. One of the Cree had saddled and tied the reins to the saddle horn of the grulla by the time he reached where his stud had been staked amongst an island of green grass in the sage. As he came alongside the animal, he made up his mind.

No highbinder Montana Territorial judge was going to hang him for something he hadn't done, and no fat sheriff was going to confiscate money he'd worked over five years to save. And, he'd had a hangman's noose rasp his Adam's apple once before, and swore then it'd never happen again.

He'd rather have it all end here and now.

13

The sheriff let down the hammers on the shotgun, remounted, and was sliding it back in the scabbard as the redhead shoved Sam up alongside the horse. A pockmarked Cree in filthy leather leggins held the horse's lead rope, with the bridle tied to the saddle horn.

As Sam swung up, he gigged the animal hard to the ribs and gave a rebel yell. "Yeehaw, gid'up, Blue." The blue grulla, never the bashful one, charged directly into the Cree, knocking him flying.

The redhead tried to hang on to Sam's leg, but with great pleasure Sam drove a left hand back time and again into the man's hatchet nose, and after three leaps, he dropped away, rolling in the dust.

Sam bent low in the saddle, grabbed up the trailing lead rope, and stayed low as a handful of chopped-up nails sliced the air over his head.

In five jumps he was in a sage lined ravine and pounding up away from the river bottom and the wide Yellowstone.

He was a long way from free, but he knew the blue grulla stud, and unless there was some horseflesh there he'd underestimated, or unless one of them got off a lucky shot, it was only a matter of time before he'd leave his attackers in the dust.

The bad news was his money belt, his weapons, and his bedroll were left behind.

But Last Chance Gulch and his brother's gold claim were up ahead of him. That was his first goal; then he'd worry about getting his money back.

His first thirty years had been fairly tough, but it looked as though they'd been a cakewalk compared to what might be ahead.

TWO

He shook the posse after two miles of hard riding.

The grulla had plenty of sand, and some of that money he'd left behind had come from running the rawboned horse against all comers.

A V of geese flew high overhead, heading south for the winter, and Sam wondered if they weren't giving him good advice. No, he decided, law or no law, he was heading to Helena to try and find his brother.

Sam knew he was more than two or three days' ride on to Bozeman, then at least that much more to Helena and his brother's claim . . . if his brother was still there. The Crazy Mountains were off to his right, the aspens and alders going yellow and red, and the larch turning golden, with Benson's Landing somewhere on to the west. At Benson's, a dozen or so miles ahead, he'd leave the river and head

be careful, as the trail ahead was near to flat at the moment, but after they passed Benson's Landing it would begin to climb, and they could spot him behind if he got too close.

After an hour he decided this bunch was rough-barked. They'd been riding hard and not slowed. He reined Blue up and let him blow, then gigged him into a fast walk. No need to kill his horse, as he figured they'd probably stop at Benson's if their horses didn't drop out from under them long before. At the crossing they could coffee up and grub down, and rest their poor stock.

And he was right.

He'd gotten off the trail well before he approached Benson's and moved to the north to a low ridge and small copse of cedars from where he could watch the landing a quarter mile below. A flatboat served as ferry and was strung on stout guide ropes across the river, at least fifty paces wide here and slow-going. Two sod-roofed rough-sawn cabins, one considerably larger than the other, a privy, and a small six- or eight-horse barn set between the river and some corrals. The corrals held a dozen horses, and he figured the posse's were among them. Sam had been here before. In fact it was as far west as he'd been in Montana Territory up to now. From here on it would be new country.

Between greasy grass and the defeat of Custer, and the subsequent surrendering of the Oglala and Crazy Horse, he'd been banging around the Judith country, staying shy of the renegade bunches, taking a few buff, and caching horns and hides all over the plains.

It was there that he met another pair of trailmen, one of whom had informed him that a couple of years back he'd met a man named Liam Stranahan up in Helena and that the man and his partner had a claim up over the mountain from Last Chance Gulch. The pair of trailmen had a team and wagon, and Sam had convinced them that they need do no hunting, but if they would provide the wagon he'd provide the hides. Sam was in a hurry to see if he could find Liam. They went from stash to stash, filling the wagon with a man's height full of hides. When they were done, Sam had no desire to make the long ride to Cheyenne where he could market the hides, particularly with winter in the wind. He sold his share to the pair at bargain prices, and they said their good-byes.

When the sun set behind the Bozeman

Pass, and the half dozen hadn't departed from the landing, Sam decided now was as good a time as any to get his goods back. He led the grulla down to the corral as soon as twilight faded, tied him, then slipped alongside the rails until he found a spot against a small meadow-grass feed stack near the privy. On the way he'd stumbled across a piece of broken fence rail, and picked the two-foot length up and slapped it against his palm, judging the weight.

It would do just fine for the plan he'd formulated.

The cabin's chimney, where Sam remembered the kitchen was located, was smoking in earnest, and he figured they were about to sit to supper. His own stomach growled like a gut-shot grizzly and he remembered he'd not had a bite since a snowshoe rabbit the night before — too busy evading, then tracking, his pursuers.

Dark fell like a curtain as the moon was late rising. Sam didn't have to wait long and soon heard footsteps. Luckily the man who headed for the privy stopped long enough to light a smoke just before he entered. The light of the match revealed it was Sheriff Thacker.

Sam smiled.

The good Lord was smiling on him.

Sam waited until the man had time to get settled in the privy and into his business, then toed over, flung the door open, and popped the wide-eyed, well-compromised sheriff a good one across his bald pate with the log.

Thacker was knocked backward against the plank wall, then tumbled forward, his pants around his ankles, and went face first into the mud.

"And a good evening to you, Sheriff Thacker," Sam said in a low voice.

Sam relieved him of his gun belt and strapped it on his own waist. Then he removed the revolver and a few shells and cast the belt aside, as he couldn't get it to strap tight enough to stay on. He knelt beside the sheriff and waited for him to stir. As soon as he did, Sam placed the muzzle of the revolver in his ear, holding him down as he tried to rise.

"You'll keep real quiet, Sheriff Thacker. A man would hate to die with his pants around his ankles and his shortcomings in plain sight."

"What you want?" the sheriff managed to mumble, not yet fully having his wits about him.

"You've got my weapons, my money, and

a good Hudson River bedroll. Far as I can figure, you're no better than those thieves you're a-chasin'."

"Let me up," he managed, his wits coming back to him.

"You're not doing the talkin' at the moment, Sheriff. It seems I'm holding the traces, and you're just along for the ride."

"Like I said, what do you want?"

"Nothin' but what's mine. Where are my goods?"

"Inside, the money's in my saddlebags and the weapons are near."

"And my bedroll?"

"Hell, we left the lice-ridden thing."

"Sit up, and keep shut-up unless you want me to blow your brains all over the shit-house wall."

"I'm not daft. I know who's holding the cards here."

Sam allowed him to roll over and come to a sitting position, his legs out in front of him. He tried to work his pants up, but Sam gave him a kick in his ample bare butt.

"Leave 'um down."

The sheriff sighed deeply. "It's cold. . . . Ain't right, coming on a man with his trousers down."

"There's a lot wrong in this world," Sam

said with a slight a chuckle.

"Now what?" the sheriff asked.

"Now we're going to move over to the main cabin, and you're gonna give a shout and call one of your boys out, tellin' him you need a hand. In fact, let's make it the redheaded one."

"Rusty?"

"Rusty's the one. I owe him a lick. Get up."

The sheriff rolled to his knees, then rose, trying to pull his pants up as he did so.

"Leave 'um down," Sam instructed.

"I can't walk —"

"You can hobble, and you will. Now, hobble your rosy-red ass over to the side wall near the window."

The sheriff grumbled with every hop of the fifty feet to the wall with the window. When they got there, Sam shoved the revolver up under the sheriff's ample chin.

"You'll do exactly as I say, understand?" Sam whispered.

"What?"

"Where are the Cree?"

"Them redskins won't come inside. They're camping out in the brush somewheres."

That worried Sam. He knew the stationmaster had only one helper, a gimpy, wisp

24

of an old man with a leg that hadn't healed right after being broken with a mule's well-placed kick. Sam knew Porky Tomlinson, the stationmaster, in passing. He was a crusty old sort, shaped like his nickname, but seemed fair to a fault. It was the Cree that worried Sam the most . . . not knowing where they were. Still, in for a penny, in for a pound.

He continued. "Call ol' Rusty out."

"Rusty! Get your ass out here. I need some help."

Sam could hear a chair slide back, then footsteps approach the window. He shoved the sheriff back against the wall as the curtain was pulled aside and light flooded out.

"What the hell, Hiram, I ain't finished eatin'."

Sam nodded at him.

"Get out here, Rusty. Now!"

The cabin door was around the corner from the window, and Sam could hear it open and then slam, then the sound of footsteps stomping their way. Sam moved to the corner and waited. As soon as the man rounded the corner, Sam said his name, "Rusty," and the redhead stopped in his tracks, then went to his knees as the butt of the sheriff's Colts cracked him between the eyes, which rolled up as if he were seeking salvation.

But his knees were as far down as he went, so Sam brought the barrel across his head. This time he was down and quiet.

The sheriff took the opportunity to try and escape around the back side of the cabin, but with his pants only halfway pulled up, he was severely impaired.

"Don't even think about it, Thacker," Sam said quietly, well before the sheriff made the back corner.

"Damn, man, at least let me get my drawers up," the sheriff replied in a harsh whisper.

"When I'm down the trail, you can get them anywhere you wish, but not until. Now get over here and call another one out."

Resignedly, the sheriff yelled at the window, "Max, you too. We need some help."

"What the hell is y'all doin' out there?" the muffled reply came from inside, then the sound of the slamming door again. The man called Max had Sam's Remington revolver stuffed into his belt.

Sam's ploy worked until he had three of them lying prone and quiet as cordwood, and the sheriff standing by the window holding up his pants. The last one, a lanky man Thacker had called "Willie," had brought Thacker's scattergun, at the sheriff's instruction, and now Sam had it in hand as well as the sheriff's revolver.

"Now, who's left in there?" Sam asked.

"Just the stationmaster and his hand."

"Where's my money and rifle?"

"Inside. Rifle's leaning against the door. Money's in my saddlebags nearby."

You got any wrist cuffs?"

"In my saddlebags."

"Let's go get them."

The three men on the ground were coming around. The redhead had managed to sit up.

"Move," Sam said, "or I'll have to give him another whack."

Again Thacker tried to pull his pants up.

"Hop," Sam said, shoving the scattergun into Thacker's gut.

"You're a no-good son of a bitch," Thacker managed, as he hopped around the corner and headed for the door.

"You're in no position to cast insults at my sainted mother."

When they reached the door, Sam shoved Thacker inside. The startled stationmaster and his hand were clearing the table, and stopped short at the sight of the sheriff's prodigious gut shining like a harvest moon in the light of a coal-oil lantern.

"What the —"

"Mr. Tomlinson," Sam said, the scattergun now shoved against the sheriff's broad backside, "I won't be botherin' you long." Sam moved to the pack and recovered the sheriff's saddlebags, the wrist irons, and his rifle. "Sheriff here has some things that belong to me."

"Back outside, Thacker." Sam backed out the doorway and motioned the sheriff to follow.

There were only three sets of wrist irons, but those were enough to shackle the four men together. With that accomplished, Sam returned to the doorway, digging into the saddlebags as he did so.

Tomlinson stood with a lever-action rifle in hand, but the muzzle pointed at the floor. Sam's newly acquired scattergun hung limply at his side.

Sam slapped a five-dollar gold piece on the table. "A loaf of that good bread you bake and a hunk of cheese . . . maybe a little jerky if you got any."

Tomlinson smiled tightly. "Never saw the like of Thacker standin' with his britches draggin' the floor," he mumbled as he set the rifle aside and gathered what

Sam had requested. He stuffed a generous supply of food into a small flour sack, then handed it to his customer. "That's too much money," he mumbled.

"You keep it for the bother. You'll have to take a cold chisel to them irons, as I'm takin' the key with me."

Tomlinson merely nodded.

Sam headed out, and to the curses of the now recovered lawmen, made his way to the corral.

He broke the scattergun apart and flung the barrels one way and the stock the other, then pulled the revolver apart and scattered it. He wasn't a thief, and wanted only what was his.

He hated to scatter Tomlinson's horses, but figured he had no choice. Dropping the gate rails to the corral, he hoorahed the horses out into the night, then mounted and drove a dozen head away as he gave Blue the spurs and galloped into the darkness.

He'd never been particularly friendly with the law, but he'd never been against it.

He figured he sure as the devil was now.

But he had his hard-earned, and his firearms. More importantly, he still forked the grulla, and they had a head start.

Three

Sam rode well into the night, letting Blue find the way.

When the moon rose he reined away from the trail and followed a trickle of a creek up a deep ravine until the trickle disappeared and he topped a small rise. When he was deep in an aspen grove, with its golden fall foliage shimmering in the moonlight, he found a small clearing and staked the horse.

For the first time he ruffled through the sack Mr. Tomlinson had stuffed full of grub, and was grateful to find a big hunk of sowbelly, hard biscuits, some dried fruit, jerky, and a loaf of fresh bread. He tore off a hunk of the bread and savored it for a while, wishing he could build a fire. But he knew it was best he didn't. He brushed up a pile of aspen leaves to use as a bed, cursing Sheriff Thacker and his men as he did so, kept his Winchester at one hand and his Remington at the other, and sank deep into the musty but comforting smell of the leaf pile, and almost as quickly, into a deep sleep.

For the second day in a row he awoke with a start, light just profiling the mountains to the east, again someone speaking to him.

"You got no bedroll, ol' coon? You look like a sorry bearkill buried under that trash."

Sam scrambled to his feet, leaves falling away, Winchester in hand. He leveled it at the man in buckskins, then realized the old fella stood with his own rifle hanging loosely. The old bear dog sitting so close to the man he might as well have been leaning on him bared his teeth, but the old man placed a wrinkled hand on the dog's head, almost waist high to the man, and he quieted. The dog was scarred up as if he'd tangled with half the bears and wolves in Montana Territory; one shredded ear hung in three pieces.

"No, lost it back down the trail," Sam managed sheepishly, lowering the rifle.

"That be a mite careless. Ain't gonna get no warmer hereabouts." The man chuckled.

"Don't imagine," Sam said, his eyes suspiciously searching the aspens for anyone else.

"I hear'd your horse whinny in the night. You cost me some sleep, worrying that a band of Cree might be after my . . . after my outfit. Got a fire going up on that rise, and a pot of coffee a-bubblin'. You got a hankerin' for Arbuckles?"

"I do," Sam managed, relaxing somewhat. "Been two days since I burned my tongue with a cup of coffee." The dog uncurled his lip and lay beside the man, still keeping his eyes fixed on Sam.

With that the man spun on his heel and started away, the dog quickly up and close at his heels, still glancing back occasionally to make sure Sam was minding his manners.

The old man was dressed in well-made buckskins the color of the darker of the golden aspen leaves, carried a brass-tacked 74 Sharps heavy-target buffalo rifle nearly as long as he was tall, and a small case of .50/70 cartridges hung under his arm. He had long straggly white-gray hair flowing out from under a fur cap. His shoulders were wrapped in a wolf-skin cape, almost the same color as his own hair. Even though he was long in the tooth, Sam had the feeling he could disappear into the woods like a will-o'-the-wisp into a pool of shadow, should the need arise.

"Should I leave the horse?" Sam managed.

"Do he drink coffee?" the old man asked over his shoulder.

"Never has," Sam said, now echoing the old man's chuckle.

"Then I'd leave him be, least until we get the nod."

Sam followed, wondering who it would be that gave the nod. At the top of the aspen grove the stand gave way to a rising rugged cliff side. Under a small overhang of rock a mud-chinked log lean-to nestled into the wall, as comfortable and natural as if it'd grown there in God's own way, and a tendril of smoke meandered out of a small stone chimney in the morning stillness. A few steps away, four Indian ponies had their heads down, each grazing on his own small pile of mown meadow hay, in a corral made three sides of logs and one of rock wall. A trickle of water worked its way out of the cliff side and some was diverted through the corral, some into a man-made rock pond outside the corral. Nearby a horse-high meadow haystack nestled against the rock wall, covered with hides to keep it dry. A few furs stretched on drying-rings of encircled river willow, and hung from the branches of the nearby aspens. In the growing light Sam could make out beaver, coon, and wolf hanging on their willow rings, a couple of bear gracing the outside walls of the little cabin, and a pile of buffalo hides nearly as high as its eaves rested near the door. All looked as if they'd been well tended.

"You been busy," Sam said, patting the stack of buff hides as the old man held the door for him. The cabin was long and narrow, with sleeping mats on either end. In the middle, tending the fire, bent a pair of Indian women.

Sam snatched his floppy-brimmed hat off.

"This here's a hungry traveler," the old man said when both women looked up.

Sam extended his hand to the old man. "I'm Sam . . ." He hesitated before giving the old man his last name. He wanted the tracks he'd left behind to evaporate like morning mist. "Up from the Mississippi a couple of hard years back."

"And I be Silas Pettibone McGraw. An old coon from Ohio, longer ago than I care to remember. And this be my wife, Talking Woman, but I calls her Mrs. McGraw, and our daughter, Mary."

Sam nodded with a smile. He thought he knew who "gave the nod." He also had trouble keeping his eyes off the girl, taller than both her mother and father, with straight fine features, raven-wing-black eyes and hair, and bulges under a finely sewn buckskin dress, in all those womanly places. Sam was taken aback, and afraid he showed it.

Mrs. McGraw, an attractive woman herself, looked at him with some suspicion, and the girl, not more than twenty, merely glanced shyly and turned away to fetch a pair of tin coffee cups.

Sam received the coffee with much gratitude. As he sipped, the old man suggested, "I got a hunk of buffalo to boil and the women will slap together some fry bread, if you're a mind to eat."

Sam surmised that some unseen signal had passed between husband and wife, and that he had passed muster, if barely. "That's kind of you, Mr. McGraw. Sure I'm not putting you out? I got to be on the trail long before the sun's over the yardarm."

"Don't get many visitors, young fella, and mighty few of the white persuasion. I'd cherish the company for a while. And I'd pride you callin' me Silas."

"I only got a short while, Silas," Sam

said. "Then I got to push on. But I do have a hunk of sowbelly back in my pack. Let me fetch my horse and you can save the buff for another time. I truly appreciate puttin' my feet by your fire, and the coffee."

"That would be a fine thing, young Sam," the old man said, and toasted him with his coffee cup. "I ain't had no Chicago chicken for a good long spell." He turned to the women. "Get out the griddle, Mrs. McGraw, we got us a treat comin'. We'll still be needin' the fry bread," he said, and got an exasperated look for his trouble as she continued her work.

"I best be fetchin' some water," the old man said, snatching up a bucket and heading for the door.

"And I'll be after the horse and hog," Sam said.

He halved the slab of sowbelly before returning with it, wrapping and repacking the portion he kept, but still shared a generous two pounds with his hosts. He gained a smile, if a tight one, from Mrs. McGraw. The woman cut it into half-inch-thick slices and soon they were crackling beside cakes of fry bread.

After removing the well-browned strips, the woman mixed a spoonful of flour into the grease, then added a cup of water, and a touch of spices.

They sat down to fried sowbelly, bread, and gravy for bread soppin'. The young girl continued to glance at Sam, quickly looking away when Sam's eyes met hers. Sam reaffirmed that she was pretty as a spring morning, a true prairie flower, and in her pagan way, would stand up beside any city woman he'd known.

"Why," old Silas said with a tooth-missing grin, "I believe Miss Mary fancies you, ol' coon." His wife gave him an exasperated chastising slap on the shoulder, and both Sam and the young girl blushed.

Sam rose when his tin plate was sopped clean. "That was fine and I thank you, Mrs. McGraw . . . and you too, Miss Mary." The woman nodded and the girl blushed, but this time with a flashing smile.

"Come on outside," Silas said, still grinning. "I don't have much left, but I'll share a chaw with you while we sit in the morning sun."

Before he moved away, Mrs. McGraw took a swatch of cloth and wiped the grease out of the old man's beard. The attention touched Sam, and he thought of his own mother for the first time in a long while. He got a catch in his throat, then shook it off. "Don't chaw, but I'll take another half cup of that Arbuckles, if you got it to spare."

The woman grabbed the pot and filled his cup; then he followed the old man outside as the women began cleaning up.

They took a seat on a pair of timber rounds in front of a spent fire. "Talking Woman doesn't talk much, does she?"

Silas smiled. "She don't . . . Says I talk enough for a whole tribe."

"Daughter Mary's a quiet one too."

"Hell, she jabbers like a jay when she gets over the bashfuls."

Sam laughed, thinking he'd like to have the chance to get her over her "bashfuls."

"Don't chaw, eh?" Silas asked, but rose at the same time and headed to the meadow haystack. He dug deep into the hay and came up with a corked pottery crock. He hurried over to Sam, uncorking with his teeth as he came, then poured a generous dollop in Sam's coffee cup, putting one finger to his lips, hushing Sam as he did so. "After a spell with the 'black robes,' and after seeing the trouble it brung her people, Talking Woman don't much fancy the whiskey. Even though it be the elixir of life to us white men, it's the devil's own brew to the red." He took a long draw

38

directly from the spout as he headed back to the haystack to bury it again. "I even had to grow the corn and work my still over in the next watershed to keep her from seein'. Damn elk and deer had the most of it et afore it came to kernel."

Sam smiled. It was a little early in the day for him, but he figured he could use it, and was pleasantly surprised when it was soft as a sow's ear, the easiest-drinking corn he'd ever tasted. He had miles of hard riding ahead of him, and figured it would do him no harm. He had the urge to tell old Silas that the brew was hardly the elixir of life to many white men, including his own pa, but held his tongue. The old man was rightly proud of his whiskey.

"So where ya off to?" Silas asked.

"West."

"We'll be headin' to winter in the Deer Lodge Valley, or maybe all the way through Hell Gate to the Bitterroot, if the weather holds long enough to get there."

"You'd leave this place?"

"We winter in the high mountains. Got us a fine place up in the Flint Creek country. Yes, siree. Plains wind bites too deep. Hell, one winter over in Judith Gap your chaw would freeze before it hit the ground and —"

"I'm headin' at least as far as Helena," Sam said, purposefully interrupting the old man, as he didn't want to get into a long, drawn-out winter story. He was beginning to get the itch to put spurs to the grulla.

"And we'll be close at yer heels. The spring will freeze up soon. This be a spring and summer place . . . not fittin' for winter."

They could see down the cut over the aspens, falling away toward the Yellowstone a couple of miles in the distance, and as Sam rose and stretched, a murder of ravens lifted out of the golden copse a half mile down the way he'd come.

Silas noticed Sam studying the disturbance of the flock of birds.

"You expectin' company?" Silas asked, turning serious, spitting a wad of chaw near his own moccasined feet.

"Could be."

"You seem a bit on the nervous side, Sam, ol' coon. You got someone doggin' your trail?"

Sam studied the old man, then decided to level with him. "I got crosswise with the Bozeman law. They think I'm someone else, and I don't have time to explain I'm not to some territorial judge who might get the urge to see how far my neck'll stretch."

"Thacker? You went against ol' Thacker's grain?" Silas grinned broadly.

"I surely did," Sam said, not seeing the humor in the fact.

Silas slapped his thighs and guffawed. "Hell, young fella, I hope you run that ol' coon all the way to Canada, and he don't find his way back. He ain't got no love lost for me neither. Far as I'm concerned, he's no better than a sodomite son of a bitch." Silas turned serious. "Fetch your horse and get back here. I got a place for y'all to lay low."

"You sure?" Sam asked. "I got no wish to get you involved . . . to invite trouble on my account. That ol' blue horse down there will run the legs off of Thacker's bunch."

"Get your horse. If that's ol' Thacker, he'll be up here lickety-split."

Sam hustled away into the trees. He saddled, then unstaked Blue. Mounting, he gigged the horse into a canter, bursting through the aspens until he reined up beside the old man.

"Follow me," Silas instructed, then led Sam up onto a rock ledge and across it for fifty yards until he came to a cleft in the wall, covered with some branches. He pulled them aside and waved Sam inside.

Mounted, Sam had to duck to get through the low, narrow opening. But when he got inside, the narrow cave broadened and he had plenty of headroom. He swung down from the grulla.

"You can stay here for a month if need be. I keep some dried things in here . . . kinda use it like a root cellar . . . and for a place to hide out if I don't like the company what's coming. Talking Woman, the girl . . . we'n used it to hide from the Cree a time or two. If'n they got mischief in mind, the devils can only come at ya one at a time. I'll come fetch you in a while, should those half-wits from Bozeman get on out of our hair."

"You sure you want to get involved in this?" Sam again asked.

"Dead sure," Silas said, giving Sam a broad grin, then explained. "Last month I took a few furs into Bozeman to trade for some necessaries. Ol' Thacker throwed me in the hoosegow for having a little taste of the local firewater . . . but all he really wanted was to fine me for most half of what I sold the skins fer. He and trader Weaver, who hangs his hat in Bozeman, are in cahoots. I have it in me to trick the fool for cheatin' me. And, hell's fire, youngster, any ol' coon who'd share his

Chicago chicken . . ."

He pushed the brush back into the opening, the light went dim, and Sam could hear him shuffle away.

He'd only been gone ten minutes or so when Sam heard the clattering of shod horses, and voices. A cackling laugh rang out, one he recognized as Thacker's deputy, Rusty Pacovsky.

Hell, had the old man given him up, led him up here only to corner him like a dog in a ditch trap?

He sure as hell wasn't leading them away.

They were coming closer.

Four

When he heard the rattle and clink of shod horses just outside the opening, Sam ratcheted back the hammer of the Winchester, expecting the brush to be dragged away and light to flood his hiding place.

Blue's head began to rise and his ears swiveled toward the sound. Sam feared he would nicker to the other horses. He quickly covered the horse's muzzle with a hard hand, and the horse stayed quiet.

Then he heard the old man's voice. "He followed this here ledge, on up to that yonder rock ledge, near that pedestal rock. Looked to me like he was trying to keep from leaving sign."

Thacker's voice echoed low and gravelly. "How far this rock go?"

"Two miles or more up the canyon," Silas said. "Hell, he coulda headed out most any way. Tolt me he was headin' back to the Musselshell. An' he was in a big hurry-up."

"You best be talkin' true, old man, or we'll be back here to split yer gullet and feed your liver to the crows."

"You say there's a reward for that ol' coon?" Silas asked.

Sam flinched. Maybe the old man was having second thoughts.

"Will be," Thacker answered, his voice beginning to fade, "soon as we get back to Bozeman and get it approved, if'n we don't catch him afore."

"Don't do me no good now. Hell's bells, I be needin' to make some money. Seems to be a fat owl-hoot cheated me out of some of my hard-earned the last time I was in Bozeman."

"Watch yer mouth, old man."

The clink of horse hooves faded, along with the voices.

In a few moments, Sam could hear the old man's harsh whisper. "You best enjoy the dark a mite longer. Make sure they's not watchin' our camp."

Sam remained silent.

It was a half hour before the old man returned.

The brush was swept away, and the old man stood eclipsing the entrance, a load of furs heaped in his arms. "We're a-packin' up, ol' coon. If you fancy it, we'll travel with you awhile."

When he dumped the pile, he selected a skin off the top and tossed it to Sam. "This one was well worked by the ladies, and will make a fine bedroll . . . better'n blankets any time."

"Obliged," Sam said, rolling the pelt and snugging it on behind the saddle. "Do we have to go through Bozeman?" he asked.

"We'll be takin' the old Indian tradin' trail, across the Crazy Woman's . . . be far north of Bozeman and south of Helena, until we come on the Missouri just below Three Forks and follow it downriver near to Helena."

"Sounds right to me," Sam said, as he figured the farther he stayed away from Bozeman, the better off he'd be. "What can I do to help?"

"Gonna cache most the furs here, and only be takin' the best to trade for winter goods."

"How long before Thacker knows he's been hoodwinked?" Sam asked, following the old man out after he stowed the furs.

"We'll be long gone. I tolt him a wee lie. That rock runs five miles or better up that draw, all the way to the summit . . . just keeps a-gettin' steeper an' steeper. He's got to check more draws and coulees than you got fingers and toes before he realizes you ain't gone thataway. But we shan't lolly-gag."

It was early afternoon before they were loaded up. To Sam's surprise, both women were mounted with small packs behind, and the other two horses were packed with heavy loads. The old man, carrying a pack at least half as heavy as that of the horses, stayed on shanks mare as they headed west. He had the lead, then Talking Woman, then young Mary, and Sam brought up the rear.

Sam figured the old man must be hided with whang leather. Tough and hard as the griddle the sowbelly was cooked on. He worked his way out of camp over another long rock ledge, then into a small stream. He was over a mile before he began to leave sign. Then he seemed not to notice that his buckskins were soaked from the knee down.

Even though the old man was confident Thacker and his band would not get wise until late in the day, Sam could not help checking his back trail each time they crested a rise.

Young Mary must have been worried too, as she kept looking back, catching Sam's admiring eye more often than not.

It was midafternoon before they took a

47

break more than just to wind the horses. And then, the old man said he was going to back-trail up to the last rise to make sure they weren't being followed.

Sam, knowing he was the only reason they might be tracked, stopped the old man and took off himself to check their back trail.

"You got some jerky in that sack?" the old man asked as Sam started to rein away.

"Yeah, you need it?" Sam asked, prepared to dig it out for his newly found friends.

"Nope, but you might gnaw some while you're watchin'. We'll take a bite here and catch our wind. You wait on the rise for an hour, then catch up. Hell, a Boston dandy could track this outfit, so you won't have no trouble."

"Suits me," Sam said, and cantered away.

He watched for at least an hour, seeing no sign of pursuers. But he'd had a taste of this bunch, and knew they could make time if they so desired. He wouldn't feel safe until he was at least three days ahead. Letting the blue grulla set his own pace, he backtracked his own trail to find his party.

Fifty miles southwest of Helena, Liam

Stranahan leaned on the intricate carved bar of the Kaiser, Phillipsburg's newest and most elite establishment. A two-story brick building catering to the miners on the way to the Flint Mountains, it was seldom quiet.

The reorganization of the Hope and the formation of the Northwest Mining Company had been the spark that revitalized the town, a town that in the sixties had been growing at the rate of one house a day.

As it was, the town boasted not only the new Kaiser Hotel, but a fine Masonic Hall, a Miner's Hall, and many commercial establishments.

Liam and his partner, Gunter Kauffmann, had just finished two dozen oysters, at six bits to the dozen, and a pair of T-bone steaks, fifty cents each. Gunter was of equal height to Liam, but Gunter was square-headed with no neck and a body as solid as the granite cliffs they hoped to mine. His hair was the color of dirty sand, kept short, and he was going bald on the crown of his skull. It was Gunter's hands most people noticed. Each hand looked like a hunk of hewn marble, ham-sized, with strong stubby fingers. Liam, like his brother, Sam, had black hair, but unlike

Sam, had warm brown eyes.

Now the two partners sipped brandy, three fingers for two bits. It was a splurge for the two of them. Since they'd sold out their claims in Grizzly Gulch, near Helena, things had not gone well. It had been Liam who had convinced his neighbor Gunter to sell out to the syndicate, that he and Gunter would do even better the next time, and Gunter had held a grudge since word got to them that the syndicate had hit it big.

Of course, Gunter gave no credence to the fact that the syndicate had poured over fifty thousand dollars into the Growler One and Berlin One, Liam's and Gunter's neighboring claims. Money that Liam and Gunter would never have had been able to raise by mining a shovel and panful at a time.

Phillipsburg, on the northern edge of the Flint Creek Valley, had been fed and nurtured by one of Montana Territory's early gold discoveries, but like many gold and silver towns, had bloomed and faded. From a onetime population of fifteen hundred, not long after the Cordova Lode silver discovery, it had faded to the number of residents that could be counted on fingers and toes, then bloomed again with new strikes and a few hard-rock mines, but not to its former glory.

And Liam Stranahan was just as happy that the town was not overrun with grubstake miners. They weren't looking for neighbors. He and his partner had made a modest discovery in the mountains to the east, the Flint Creek Range, on a trickle they'd christened Siglinda Creek after Gunter's mother. And the twenty-acre claims were called, at Gunter's insistence, Siglinda One and Two. Siglinda Creek was giving up color, but not enough to yield the two of them over a few dollars a day.

But Liam had faith in the find, and was dead-set certain that they'd find a mother lode somewhere in one of the ravines feeding the creek. And a hard-rock mine was in the offing . . . if they could but find the vein that fed the creek.

Now, each of them sipped a brandy and eyed the other. There was no hint of a smile on either man's face. It was obvious to the bartender they were partners, but not necessarily friends.

Gunter, by far the most serious of the two, had been pestering Liam to break up the partnership, and had offered, time and time again, to buy Liam out. Liam was more than willing to sever their relationship, and each time Gunter had made the offer, had in turn reversed the flow of things . . . offering Gunter the same amount if he would be the one to sell.

It was a standoff, and the smoldering pot of disagreement was slowly coming to a boil.

"Humph," Gunter groaned. "They be no damned mother lode, you Irish fool. We're scrapin' up the last of it, grubbin' it out of that muddy trickle."

"Muddy?" Liam challenged. "Hell, that's as fine and pure a little creek as the likes of you will ever see, Gunter, me lad. And it's an insult to yer fine old ma to say otherwise."

"Humbug. I am gonna make you one last offer, Stranahan. I vill gif you one thousand dollars, cash money, for you interest in the claims. I vant to build a house there, and to bring a woman from the East."

Liam eyed him, knowing he was lying. But Liam only smiled, which seemed to make Gunter angry.

"That seems a bit too much to me," Liam said, "but like always . . . likewise, I'll give you a thousand for your interest."

Gunter reddened, then stomped away, leaving his unfinished brandy on the bar.

"What's good for the goose . . ." Liam called after him.

"What's got a bug up his backside?" Tom Beauchamp, the tall, thin bartender, asked.

Liam looked up at the man, and gave him a smile. "Hell, Gunter's been belly-aching about something ever since I knowed him. Maybe it's the German way."

Beauchamp mopped the bar with a rag. "He finished with that?" He motioned to the half-full glass Gunter had left.

Liam reached over and picked it up, pouring the remaining brandy in his own glass. "He is now."

"Where'd ol' Gunter stomp off to?"

"Betsylou's, I'd guess."

Betsylou Maddigan ran the newly opened brothel in town. She'd brought four girls with her from Helena and was looking to hire more, and both Gunter and Liam had known her and some of her girls well.

In fact, one of the girls had worked her way into a soft spot in Liam's heart. She called herself Helen, but Liam knew that wasn't her real name. Miss Maureen O'Toole's family was from county Cork, not far from where Liam's own had originated. If only she hadn't been a soiled dove, Liam would have squired her away long ago. But he just couldn't bring himself . . .

Still and all, after he finished his brandy — and the rest of Gunter's — he'd probably find his way to Betsylou's. It seemed he couldn't come to town without doing so.

Liam took a deep drink, saddened at his partner's desire to get shed of him, and saddened even more that the only woman he'd ever had a deep feeling for was a whore.

Sam was surprised how far ahead of him the McGraws were. He'd come almost three miles, and was deep in a stand of lodgepole, following the trail that was not much more than a game track, when he heard the popping sounds.

He reined up, and listened.

No doubt about it, gunfire. And it was up ahead of him. Up where the McGraws must be. He knew both the women had old needle guns, and the old man his big-bored Sharps. The old needle guns were cap-and-ball muzzleloaders, older than Sam, and slower than honey on a December morning. And the old man's rifle was a cartridge-fed breechloader, but it was single shot. He was good for six or seven rounds a minute, and the women maybe two. And the gunfire was coming a lot faster than that.

Hell, they must be under attack.

He gave the spurs to Blue, pounding through the forest, taking the slap of pine boughs. It was a quarter hour of hard riding before he reached the spot, knowing he was there because some of the contents of the packs were strewn about.

And worse, Silas's old dog lay shot dead.

Silas, the women, and the horses were nowhere to be seen.

But the tracks of another dozen unshod horses were in plain sight.

And there was a blood trail, leading off toward the north with the track of a whole band of horses. At least there were no bodies left behind.

Thacker? No, the horses were unshod, and there were surely more than a half dozen. And the shod ponies of the Mc-Graws were mixed with them.

It had to be a band of renegade Indians.

Sam took a deep breath. Hell, as if he didn't have enough trouble already. But the McGraws had treated him decently. And the fact was, he sure as hell couldn't let the old man, Mrs. McGraw, and particularly young Mary fall into the hands of a bunch of savages. If he let that happen it would grate on his backbone for all time.

He was only minutes behind them. But what the hell would he do when he caught up?

He hesitated only a moment as the thoughts assailed him, then again put the spurs to the stud.

One man against a dozen . . .

Five

Blackfeet, Piegans, and Bloods . . . all cousins, all feared on the plains.

Sam had been tested by all of them at one time or another, had lost gear and hides to them, and been put afoot by them once. He'd kept a Piegan brave from lifting his hair by shoving the Remington deep in his belly and lighting the linsey-woolsey shirt, one he'd probably stolen from some settler, afire with the muzzle blast.

Sam had kept his hair, and had no interest in taking the Indian's.

Mrs. McGraw was full-blooded Indian, old Silas had said, Blackfeet. Would the cousin tribes harm her? Or her daughter?

Then again this bunch could be Cree or even Shoshoni, the historical enemies of the Blackfeet.

Sam dogged their trail over a small crest, then could see far ahead as the trail dropped away to follow the west slope of the Crazies north. The blood trail had stopped, and no body had been cast aside, so Sam figured whoever it was had at least quelled the bleeding.

He followed at a leisurely pace until late in the afternoon, when the trail turned up a deep canyon. He took his time as there was no sense catching up with the bunch while they were mounted. He had to wait until they settled into a night camp, or until they returned to some camp they'd left behind to go on their raid.

Sam thought he detected smoke in the distance, where the canyon rose to the foot of the timberless cliffs that climbed high out of the lodgepole pine. There was probably a glacier lake in a bowl at the top of the canyon, a good place to camp. But the smoke could merely be afternoon mists.

One thing he knew for sure: he couldn't follow blindly along their trail. They would surely leave a man watching their back trail as they neared camp. Sam studied the lay of the land, then decided he would cut through the copse of lodgepole until he reached the timberline, then work his way along it until, with luck, he could see down into the bowl and into their camp.

The afternoon clouds were building over the mountaintops, and it smelled like rain, or snow. Sam could see his breath, and the grulla's, which boded well for snow. When he topped out of the trees, he could definitely see a column of smoke a mile in the distance. When he got within a half mile, he staked Blue in a small meadow and made his way on foot.

Eight or ten teepees set on the edge of a still lake, the east side of which was a vertical granite wall, the west side a meadow where the Indian camp had been made, then a thick grove of aspens. High above on the peaks the snow had already settled in for the winter. Two snow-fed creeks and a waterfall nourished the lake, the creeks coming in from the north and south along steep beds lined with willows, the waterfall from the high granite cliff. A much larger drain creek wandered through the meadow and the teepees, then dropped off through the aspens and into a dark forest of lodgepoles and firs.

Under different circumstance, it would have been a pastoral scene.

Sam hunkered down in the willows alongside the most northerly feeder creek, and watched the camp, a quarter mile below. The good news was the camp was made up of women, children, and old folks. It wasn't only warriors. On the far side of the meadow two dozen horses grazed. Among them Sam thought he recognized the McGraws' string.

He couldn't do anything in full light, so he stayed deep in the willows and waited. He wouldn't have long, as the granite cliffs were already going from cold gray to gold with the setting sun.

Betsylou's Saloon and Sporting Establishment was actually hardly more than a brothel, but was a two-story affair, the fine house of a former successful miner who'd fallen on hard times. Betsylou had brought the run-down house back to not overly fancy, as brothels go, but substantial. It sat at the top of Broadway, on the crown of a small hill, near the wall of lodgepole pine that marked the beginning of the forest, well beyond the fine houses belonging to a couple of the hard-rock mine owners, a prominent local cattleman who could look over his stock in the valley below, and a merchant who ran the mercantile. Each of the four girls had her own room upstairs and Miss Betsylou had a suite of rooms on the bottom floor, in the rear, behind the kitchen. The drawing room and dining room had been converted to the social area, where customers could get a look at the girls, a drink, and maybe even a free dance if the piano player was on duty. The men paid twice as much for a drink as they did at the Kaiser, but didn't seem to mind as the company was much more obliging. And it was here that they purchased a one-dollar token from Betsylou, which they would give to the girl of their choice in return for a visit to her room. The girl would give her tokens to Betsylou at the end of the night in return for fifty cents each.

Commerce, at its simplest and most straightforward, and in one of its oldest forms.

Liam arrived just as the sun ducked behind the mountains across the Flint Creek Valley. Dismounting the tall buckskin he rode, he tied the horse to the rail. He had tarried at the Kaiser to finish another drink, one bought for him by the bartender, Tom Beauchamp. He was a little tipsy as he negotiated the ten stairs up to the front porch. It was beginning to get a little nippy, and no one occupied the half dozen wicker chairs lining the broad porch.

It was, however, reassuring that the red lantern near the door was already aglow.

Only a half dozen men, none of whom Liam knew, and three girls occupied the social rooms. He did know the lone China-man at one of the tables, playing solitaire; One-Eyed George Choi was a celebrity of sorts in Phillipsburg. Helen was not in attendance in the social rooms when he arrived. A little twinge of jealously raised the temperature on the back of his neck, knowing she must be up in her room with another customer.

Damn fool, he thought to himself as he sauntered over to the small bar and ordered three fingers of brandy. As he studied the red velvet pattern on the walls, he decided, *Her business is her business!*

He hadn't yet had time to take a sip when Betsylou Maddigan sidled up to him, nestling one of her large breasts against his biceps.

"Mr. Liam Stranahan, it's been a month of Sundays. . . ."

"Not all that long, Miss Betsylou," Liam said, glancing down at her rouge-covered face, giving her a wink. "We were down the mountain just a month ago."

"I do recall. You got a moment?" she asked, batting her long eyelashes at Liam, then motioning him into the rear. This silenced and surprised the crowd, as all knew that Miss Betsylou did not offer her own affections to the customers, but only

e loads in his Remington re-
made sure he had extra car-
is pockets. He'd already loaded
ester fully and cleaned it, using
our-segment cleaning rod stored
k. He had one more chore, and
the four parts of the rod and re-
the stock.

ime. Full dark, and the moon
e up for a couple of hours.

he was going into the lion's
e had no choice . . . at least no
choice.

those of her girls. Which was fine with Liam, as her ample figure and bulging bosom were not particularly to his taste, and besides, it would hurt Miss Helen's feelings. But he liked Betsylou a lot.

He obliged and followed Miss Betsylou through the dining room, where a loud cribbage game was under way on the dining room table. It too quieted as Liam followed the woman by the boisterous men and into the kitchen, then beyond, to her private rooms.

Betsylou cautioned him, making sure he didn't get the wrong idea. "This ain't business, at least not such as is carried on here," she said, as soon as her door had closed behind him. They were in another sitting room, with its own outside door onto a back porch. Liam presumed the door beyond was her bedroom, but she made no move to it.

"Oh," Liam said. "We just havin' a visit?"

"Nope, take a seat, and I'll tell you what this is about."

Liam did as instructed, lowering himself into a deep upholstered chair and taking a sip from the brandy snifter he'd brought with him. She pulled a ladderback chair away from the wall and sat near him, lowering her voice.

"Liam, I heard some things earlier I don't think I was meant to hear, and they concern you."

This perked Liam's ears up. "And just who was doin' the talkin'?" Liam asked.

"One was your partner. I could tell by the accent. I didn't see the other man. But I can tell you, they were up to no good. They were out on the porch, and I'd pulled the top casement window down a smidgen to let the smoke out."

"Concerning me?"

"If you're the fella who'll be taking the east road up the mountain tonight, then it's concerning you."

"So, what was said?"

"Something, in a German accent, about one hundred dollars if the man on the road, riding a buckskin horse, is shot cold dead, and that man proves to be Liam Stranahan. And the shooter gets to keep the horse."

That silenced Liam for a moment as he tried to absorb what she'd told him. Then he mumbled, "The son of a bitch."

"He's always been that, at least when it came to the girls. I have no idea about the rest of his business."

"You're certain it was Gunter, and certain he was talking

"Liam, my love, only heard, but I tomers tonight wi the man definitely you?"

"That's me." H then again turned old Gunter wanted but I had no idea

"Just be carefu warned."

"Thank you, Be than I can say."

"Just keep brin And be careful, s on back before t wrong idea and st

Liam managed followed her out.

Both Gunter an others in the roon been the one she angered Liam aln he'd hired someon a dog.

Sam checked t making sure the l ning knife he ca

checked volver a tridges i the Win the small in the st unscrewe stored it

It was wouldn't

He kn jaws, but honorabl

Six

Gunter, standing near the small bar with a couple of men, said nothing to Liam while he finished his brandy. Finally, after Liam stood watching the cribbage game for a while, Gunter walked over.

"I'll be stayin' in town tonight," the German growled, "so I won't be ridin' home with you."

"Suit yourself," Liam said, barely looking up from the game. "Ain't the best trail to be on in the dark of night." Liam glanced at him, barely able to contain his contempt. "I'll be leaving after a couple more of these brandies to keep me warm on the way home."

"Humph," was all Gunter managed, turning to leave. He stopped short, then asked, "You sure you won't be sellin' me your interest?"

Liam laughed aloud, then countered, "I'll be buyin' you out, not the other way around . . . or maybe I'll just have to out-live you."

With that, he got a strange look from the big German; then the man shrugged and shouldered his way to the door and left without glancing back.

As soon as he was gone, Liam crossed the room to where Helen, as tired as she would be had she worked her way through a regiment of soldiers, stood visiting with Betsylou.

"Miss Helen," Liam said, his hat in hand, "what would it cost me to take your time for the rest of the night?"

Helen eyed him with sad eyes. "It would be my pleasure to have your company, Liam Stranahan, for the cost of one slim token until the morning sun." She glanced at Betsylou for confirmation, then added, "It's late, and these louts have all been well worked over."

"You'll get no argument from me," Betsylou said, patting Helen on the shoulder.

Helen eyed Liam and almost pleaded, "You'll be givin' me a little time to sleep?"

"It's sleep and a safe warm bed I'm seekin'," Liam said, his own voice suddenly echoing a deep exhaustion, and a little sadness.

"I'm thinkin' we could all use a little sleep," Betsylou said. "I'll be takin' my leave." She placed a hand on Liam's shoulder, and said quietly, "I'm sorry about your partner, Liam."

"It's him you should be sorry for," Liam said, suddenly letting his sadness give way to anger.

Deciding he'd let Gunter's shooter spend a cold night waiting for his quarry, and deal with it in the fresh cold light of morning, he excused himself and went out and put his horse up in Betsylou's small barn.

When he returned, he found Helen in her room, cleaning herself up with a washcloth at the white porcelain bowl and pitcher. She was as naked as God had made her, and as lovely a woman as Liam had ever seen. Normally, she performed her job in a nightgown, and it was the first time he'd seen her as God had created her.

He thanked God for the pleasure, pulled his boots off and stripped down to his long johns, and climbed into the soft feather bed.

It had been a good night's sleep he wanted, but the sight of her changed his mind.

Sam lay quietly in the shelter of the willows for at least two hours, then afraid the moon would rise and give up too much light for what he had in mind, he set out.

He had no trouble making his way toward the camp. The Indians had built a huge fire in its center and were all gathered there. At least, he hoped all.

Still he was very cautious in his approach, making sure of every footfall, not allowing the smallest snap of a twig. It took the better part of a half hour to cover the quarter mile down the stream. When he was thirty yards from the nearest teepee he had to leave the streambed and the cover of the willows. An owl swooshed low overhead and startled him so badly it took a moment to catch his breath.

The Indians were beginning to get loud, and he could see them passing a couple of McGraw's crocks around. Whiskey. The old man must have had a pair of whiskey crocks hidden in his packs.

The old reprobate may have a big thank-you coming from Mrs. McGraw for his whiskey habit, should these Indians get drunk enough to pass out. That was something to consider, as far as his visit to their camp was concerned. But then again, the moonrise was more important. If he was successful in freeing them, should any of them be alive, the dark night would be their best ally.

Before he approached the tent he noticed the remuda of free-grazing horses between the camp and the lake. He slipped back into the willows, worked his way back up the creek forty or more yards, then moved away and into the grazing animals until he found what he thought were the McGraws' stock, among what must have been a hundred head. Then he noticed a few horses tied to a picket line. He knew it was the habit of the Indians to tie their better horses, the prime riding stock, and not let them wander. The first thing he did was cut the ties of each of the best horses. Each of the McGraw horses wore a headstall, making them easy to find. He had no lead ropes, but took the animals, one at a time, and led them to the outside of the band, as close as he could get them to the camp.

As he made his way back, he noticed a pile of tack, and found some ropes and returned to the McGraw stock and tied the lead ropes to their headstalls, letting them drag them so they'd be easy to catch.

Then he again moved toward the encampment. In the inky night he almost stumbled across the old man's naked body, staked out on the ground, arms and legs spread and stretched taut.

He dropped to his belly and crawled up to where he could whisper and be heard. "Silas." The old man didn't move . . . maybe didn't breathe.

Then he groaned quietly, pulling against his restraints.

"Silas. Keep quiet. It's Sam."

Slowly, the old man opened his eyes, and turned his head. The only appendage he could move. "Sam? Sam who?"

"Sam Stranahan, you old fool."

"Sam . . . Saw me loose, Sam. Get me outta here."

Sam noticed then that the old man had been beaten badly. His body was criss-crossed with welts and scabs. "What the hell did they do to you?"

"Damned old women had their fun. Not hurt bad, 'cept'n one old hag whacked me with a rock and cracked my melon. They got more planned later, if'n I know my Bloods."

Sam jerked the skinning knife and with four swipes had the old man's rawhide bindings cut away.

"They come check on me ever once in a while," he managed, as he sat up, rubbing his bloodless wrists. Then he pointed with a trembling finger. "Mrs. McGraw and Mary are over in that teepee."

"Guarded?" Sam asked.

"Doubt it, probably bound. They's all having a hoora with my good whiskey, gettin' of a mind to roast me over that big fire, I imagine."

"I'm gonna go see if I can get the women out," Sam said.

"You ain't goin' without me," Silas managed, trying to get to his feet.

"Ain't the way it's gonna be, Silas," Sam said, helping him up. "Two will make twice the fuss as one. You go over to the herd. I got lead ropes on your four nags. Gather 'em up so we can light a shuck out of here."

Silas was quiet for a moment, studying the situation. Then he sighed. "You're probably callin' it right." Then he hesitated. "I'd be a lot more inclined to hang back, should I have that rifle. Besides, should they give you the chase, I can scatter 'em."

"You shot a lever action?"

"I shot 'em all, son. Let's get goin' afore they come lookin'. That's old Hunting Hawk's teepee. It's buff cowhide, hair on the outside, and a layer of elk skin underneath. Don't try slicin' through the buff, peel it back. You can cut that elk hide with one swipe, with that little pig sticker of your'n."

Sam handed him the rifle.

Silas moved away, his naked body white in the starlight.

Sam shook his head in amazement at the old man.

Now for the hard part. The teepee was thirty yards from where they had staked the old man out. When he was content with the whoopin' and hollerin' coming from around the big fire, Sam slipped a little farther out into the darkness and made his way until most of the Indians were hidden from view behind the big teepee, and he was in its fire shadow. As stealthily as he could, he eased up to the teepee, staying hidden in the darkness.

As instructed, Sam quietly found an overlap and peeled the layer of furred buff hide back until the well-weathered dark brown elk skin was exposed. He had no idea who was in the teepee. Old Hunting Hawk, whoever the hell that was, could be in there worrying the women. Silently, he slipped the point of the knife through the elk hide, made a two-inch cut, then leaned against one of the tent poles and hunkered forward so he could get his eye up to the hole. Enough light found its way into the tent from the flap, facing the fire, that he could see. Luckily only the two women were there. They lay tied, on either side of a still fire, its embers glowing softly.

Very, very carefully, Sam used the gut hook of the skinning knife to widen the gap until he could struggle through.

Mrs. McGraw lifted her head. Mary seemed to be asleep.

"Quiet," Sam said softly, putting a finger to his lips in the universal sign for silence.

He slipped over to the older woman's side and quickly cut away her bindings on both hands and ankles. Then he moved to Mary. As he began to cut away her restraints, she suddenly awoke, cried out, and grabbed his wrists. Her mother leaped to her and covered her mouth, whispering to her.

Sam moved to the flap and peeked out.

"An old woman is coming," he said quietly to Mrs. McGraw.

She moved to the flap, pushing him back and slipping his revolver out of its holster at the same time.

Sam started to complain, as it wouldn't do to fire the weapon with over a dozen drink-crazed braves dancing around forty or fifty feet away, but then he thought better. As hard as it was, he backed off and let her handle it.

They waited quietly. The old woman stuck her head inside, only to have Mrs. McGraw grab her by a braid and jerk her all the way into the tent, smacking her soundly with the butt of the revolver at the same time. It took one more crack before the old woman lay still on the buffalo robes covering the floor of the teepee. Mrs. McGraw gave Sam a satisfied look, then peeked outside, and when satisfied, handed the revolver back to Sam.

Mary was gathering up some of their things and bundling them. Both women hoisted a bundle, and Mrs. McGraw found the Sharps and an old U.S. Army cartridge case among some things in a pile. She handed the rifle to Sam and looked expectantly at him.

He checked the load in the rifle, then moved to the slit and slipped out into the shadow. The women handed out their bundles, then followed.

They moved quickly across the meadow to the horses, and found that Silas had them all saddled, including the pack animals.

Sam helped the women mount after they stowed their bundles in the packhorses' panniers, then moved to where Silas had mounted one of the packhorses. Sam traded rifles with Silas and handed him the cartridge case, then instructed, "Silas, give me ten minutes to get back to my horse, then whoop it up and drive these critters away so those louts can't give chase."

"Take the women with you," Silas said, and Sam nodded.

He made his way away, toeing, the sucking at the mud of the horses' hooves the only sound.

They hadn't made a hundred feet up the slope when the tone of the yelling Indians changed from hoorah to what-the-hell. Sam glanced back to see them all converging on the teepee where the women had been held. Sam broke into a run and the women gave heels to their horses. He grabbed the tail of a passing mount, and now he only hit the ground with every third pace. As Sam ran, he heard the rumble of several hundred horse hooves, and glanced back to see the Indian herd being driven directly through the camp.

Indians scattered in every direction, one of them scrambling to drag old Silas out of the packsaddle as he pounded behind the charging herd. Sam smiled as the old man dropped low in the saddle and whacked the brave away with the heavy barrel of the buff gun; then he was surprised to see the old man's horse spin back. He was reining with the lead rope in one hand, carrying the rifle in the other. He pounded the horse's flanks with his bare heels, dropped the lead rope, and aimed and fired as he charged forward. Sam could not make out what he was after, but then a volley of shots rang out from the camp. The Indians had recovered their own arms.

Sam expected to see Silas blown out of his spot on the horse's back, but the old man only dropped low with his head alongside the animal's neck, and reined away from the camp, adeptly handling the lead rope, his only rein, following their path up the hill.

Sam levered as fast as he could, and fired a half dozen shots at the camp, letting the Indians know they had a fight if they followed, then doubled his pace up the rocky slope until he reached the grulla. He jerked the stake and mounted, gathering his lead rope as he pounded away, the women on his heels, the old man now only thirty or forty yards behind.

They rode hard for twenty minutes, until Sam decided it was time to rest the horses, and he pulled up on the crest of the slope.

As the horses rested, he tried to listen for the sounds of pursuit.

Nothing.

"You better get something on," Sam said to the old man, but Mrs. McGraw was already pulling one of the bundles from a pannier on a packhorse, and digging out his clothes.

As soon as he was dressed, they moved away, this time at a rapid walk.

Riding all night, finally helped by the rising moon, they didn't dismount until they reached the shores of the Shields River and the sun peeked over the Crazy Woman Mountains, now behind them.

Crossing the river, Sam and the McGraws camped on a rise where they could see at least two miles across the valley to the east. The Big Belt Mountains were in front of them, snow-topped, a deep golden where aspens lay, dark as black satin where the pines gathered, but welcoming in the sunrise.

They ate jerky and brewed a pot of coffee over a tiny fire, and then Sam took the first watch while the others slept.

It was all he could do to keep awake, but the thought of the old man staked out, naked and beaten, offered all the encouragement he needed.

After three hours or so the old man awoke and motioned for Sam to unroll the buff belt the old man had given him. "You sure?" Sam asked. But that was all that was said as the old man poured himself a cup of coffee, picked up the Winchester, and perched himself on a rock.

He is truly a tough old hide, Sam thought as he worked his way into the bedroll in the morning sun, *even if he doesn't have as much of that ol'hide as he used to.*

Sleep came easy, with old Silas on watch.

Liam Stranahan had awakened that morning to Betsylou's admonition, "Get up, you two lazybones. We got housework to do around here before we get more customers." Her voice was harsh, but she carried a tray with coffee and a pile of cinnamon sweet bread. Leaving them on a small table near the bed, she excused herself.

Liam sat up, feeling as good as he'd ever felt, after sleeping in a fine feather bed with a beautiful woman at his side. Then he remembered his partner.

As he sipped the coffee and watched Helen, now adorned in a pink lace French frilly thing, sitting at the dressing table, brushing out her long auburn hair, he wondered what his next move might be. He hoped the hired gun his partner had employed had taken the croup and died in the night, and with luck maybe his partner also, but he knew that wasn't likely.

"What's on your devious Celtic mind?" Helen asked.

"Same as always," Liam teased, looking her up and down, not wanting to bother her with his troubles.

"You got your dollar's worth, Mr. Stranahan, so it'll be another token for another roll in the feathers."

"And more than a dollar's worth it was. You're a fine lass, Miss Helen . . . or should I say Miss Maureen O'Toole?"

She paused in her brushing and eyed him ruefully. "I don't know why I ever told you my real name. I don't even ever think it, while I'm in this place, worrying that my old ma and da would roll over under the good green sod of Ireland."

"I was thinkin' of asking you to change it," he said, letting his emotions overrule his good sense for a moment.

With this, she turned and faced him, placing the brush back on the dresser, folding her hands in her lap. It was a long moment before she replied.

"And just what does that mean, Liam Stranahan?"

He walked to the window, still in his long johns, and stared out. All the leaves had left the trees, and frost covered the porch roof below the window. "Don't much matter what it means, if it means anything . . . at least not until I get this little matter of my partner wantin' me dead settled up."

She sighed and went back to her brushing, watching him in her mirror as she did so. "Why don't you go to the town marshal?"

"And tell him what? That my partner and I are having a disagreement? That Miss Betsylou heard someone talk about shootin' me out of the saddle? But didn't know for sure who. . . . Hell, he'd just shrug and tell me to come see him after I done been shot. Which would be a hard thing, being toes up, or bear fodder in some ravine."

"Then what are you going to do?" she asked, pausing again.

"I'm going to get dressed and go over to the Kaiser for a plateful of side pork and eggs. You care to join me?"

"In public?"

"Of course, in public. When did I ever

make you think I wouldn't be proud to be seen with you in public? We've all done things we had to in order to get by, Miss Helen, but that don't mean we're not prideful, or not deserving. I think you're one of the most deserving ladies I've had the pleasure to know."

"Why, you never did tell me any such thing, Liam. And the fact you have now speaks well for you, in my way of thinking."

For a second he thought she might accompany him; then her look darkened.

"But I must be mindful of the chores I have to do, as you heard Miss Betsylou say."

"Then I'll see you next time I'm down the mountain."

"I hope so."

With that, he dressed.

As he was leaving, she called out to him. "Be careful, Liam Stranahan. I don't want to be losing you."

He tipped his hat, and closed the door.

As he crossed the rear yard on his way to the barn, he heard the casement window slide up, then her voice ring out from her second-story window. "You be careful, you hear?"

He waved over his shoulder.

He decided he would put on a good feed, buy a couple more boxes of shells, and head up the mountain the hard long way, via what was hardly more than a game trail in the next canyon over — but the way no bushwhacking shooter would be waiting.

Then he might just surprise Gunter and confront him with what had been heard at Miss Betsylou's.

That should get the firecrackers to popping. At least it would be one on one, with both of them facing each other.

He rode directly to the hostler's barn, Vandermer Livery. He knew the man not only worked for the express company, but also served as a farrier, wheelwright, and blacksmith, and he would have something Liam had decided he needed. When he entered, the barrel-chested Dutchman, Erik Vandermer, stopped pumping his bellows and called out, "Liam, my friend, does your buckskin need some work?"

"No, Erik, it's a bit of oil I need . . . or grease."

"I have both."

"Grease."

Erik motioned him to a small keg. Liam pulled his revolver from its holster, removed the belt, dipped a hand into the keg, and got two fingers full, then began working the inside of the holster with the grease.

"You lookin' to have to jerk that iron?" Erik asked, his look one of concern.

"You never know, you just never know. What do I owe you?"

"Not a penny. Just bring the buckskin back the next time he needs shoeing."

Liam strapped the rig back on his hip, then tried his draw a couple of times.

"Better," he mumbled, and spun on his heel, then hesitated. "Erik, I'll be bringing the buckskin back. Thanks."

"Don't mention," the big man said, and watched in wonder as Liam strode away.

On the way to the Kaiser, he thought of another piece of business that needed attention, and drew rein at the stage stop, which also doubled as the post office. He knew Parker Willingham, who served as both stationmaster and postmaster, and knew the officious little man had a fine hand, and would have a pen, and a sheet of paper. And, for a small fee, he would be willing to serve as witness.

There was something he wanted done, before he found himself in the middle of a gunfight.

Something that he suddenly considered couldn't be put off.

Seven

Sheriff Hiram Thacker enjoyed ham steak about as much as any man, particularly how it was prepared at Bozeman's finest restaurant in the President Madison Hotel — fried crisp on the outside. Particularly since the hotel cut Hiram's steak twice as thick as the normal one. Being sheriff did have its advantages.

Across from him sat one of the most powerful men in the territory, Judge Horace Talbot, dressed as usual in a fine city suit with a cutaway coat and four-in-hand silk tie. Talbot, too, enjoyed his vittles, but his gout had been giving him fits, and now, at the sawbones's insistence, he dined on a bowl of stewed dried apples, no sugar added. He was not particularly pleased watching Thacker sop up the last of his gravy with a fat roll and stuff it into his mouth. Then he downed the last of a quart of buttermilk, leaving a mustache of white on his upper lip, which he mopped away with the back of his hand.

"Hiram, I don't know how one man can eat so damned much."

The sheriff patted his prodigious belly. "Nothing to it, Judge. You should see me when I'm really on my feed. Hell, I could —"

Talbot held up his hand, silencing him. "Let's talk about more important things. So, you lost the trail of those murdering thieves?"

One of the last things in life he wanted to have happen was for Judge Talbot to find out that some hooligan made him hop around with his pants on his ankles, and he'd sworn the other men to secrecy — on threat of being horsewhipped.

"We followed 'em down the river and up into the Crazies. Lost the trail of two of them a few miles past Benson's Crossing. But we were able to track one of them on up into the mountains. Lost him up in the rocks." Thacker waved the waiter over. "Bring me a couple of pieces of apple pie."

Talbot shook his head in wonder, then continued, "I heard you jumped one of them in his camp."

Hiram eyed him for a long moment. "True enough. But he lit out like he could see you a-tyin' the thirteen turns in his new hemp necktie."

"And you lost him."

Hiram looked a little sheepish for a moment, then turned his attention to more important things as the waiter set a quarter of a pie in front of him.

Judge Talbot continued, as relentless as if he were interrogating a witness when he had been a prosecutor in St. Louis. "One man, ran off and left the six of you?"

"We'll get him . . . we'll get him. Thought you might want to turn loose some of that territorial money for a reward?"

"Hell, you had him, now I got to pay for him. Seems to me it would have been cheaper just to keep him."

Hiram reddened a little. "Son of a bitch had the fastest horse I ever saw. How much you willin' to offer? The good of it is, we got his name. Sam Stranahan."

"All right, all right," Talbot relented. "I'll offer a hundred dollars. Just get him, so I can try him and hang him, if need be."

"You think we can get the stage company to add a little to that?"

"I'll drop by and talk to Haggarty after lunch. You stop by the newspaper and give them a description for the handbills, but

88

tell them to hold up until I tell them how much."

"I'll do that, Horace."

After visiting the newspaper office, Thacker headed straight to his office, slamming through the door. Rusty Pacovsky dropped his booted feet to the floor, then stood up from the sheriff's chair.

"Get your ass away from my desk," Thacker growled at his deputy.

Rusty moved away slowly, then leaned on the door separating the office from the cells, scratching his ruffled red head. "What's bit your backside?"

"You! You dumb pig humper. You told Judge Talbot about us roustin' that ol' boy up on the Yellowstone, and him gettin' away. We got a big ol' smear of egg on our faces."

"Hell, boss, he asked me about it."

"What did he ask?"

Again Rusty scratched his head. "He asked me what we found while we was trackin'."

"You are dumber than a rusty anvil, Rusty Pacovsky. Just 'cause he asked don't mean you have to blabber. . . . Hell, now we got a handbill going out for the wrong man."

Rusty shrugged, then raised an eyebrow

and looked as clever as it was possible for him to look. His voice took on a conspirator's tone. "That ain't so bad, now, is it, Hiram?"

The sheriff took his chair and leaned far back. Then he let the chair drop with a plop and dug in a desk drawer for the fixin's, rolled himself a cigarette, sealed it with a lick, lit it, took a deep draw, then let the smoke drift out. "I guess it ain't so bad. But I still don't want you talking to the judge about nothing what happens in this office. Understand?"

"Sure, boss. Sure. Hell, we shoulda kept after him when we was hot on his trail."

Thacker ignored that, as it had been he who led the others back to Bozeman. He knew Stranahan had nothing to do with the robbery, and who did, and knew they were on a wild-goose chase just for show. And besides, he wasn't about to explain any of it to Pacovsky, who well knew already.

"You find Little Ears and Charley Mad-in-the-Morning, and make sure they're sober and ready to go when I give the nod. I paid Hutchins and Pendergast off last night with their share and sent them on their way, so it's just you and the Cree —"

"They was good men —"

"And they greased their gullets with a lot of whiskey. It was either pay them off and send them packin', or give them the same medicine your brother got. Anyways, they're long gone. The McGraws' trail lit out to the west from the old man's camp, and the more I think on it, I got a hunch that Stranahan fella is riding with old man McGraw. It would be just like that old hard case to feed us a pile of bull."

"And we're going after 'em?"

"No, you and the Cree is going after 'em. I got business here."

"That means I get the reward? And hell, I might just get a crack at that young half-breed of ol' man McGraw's."

"You keep your pants latched. An' don't be shootin' the old man unless he gets his hackles up and you ain't got no choice. Now, what it means is you get two dollars a day, and you get half the reward if you bring him in, breathin' or stone cold, and you pay the Cree."

"Ain't right."

"Nothin' much is. Go find your trackers."

"Ain't right."

"Look, Rusty, it was your brother what got kilt, and it'll look better if'n you are the one hot on the killer's trail."

"The son of a bitch needed killin'."

"Don't get me started. . . . I told you I didn't want anyone kilt. I just wanted the ol' boy shot up a little so's he couldn't run for sheriff. Shootin' him dead center in the wishbone wasn't what I had in mind."

Rusty ignored that, but continued, "I'll go, but the whole reward oughta be mine, not your'n and mine . . . and those Cree can take the hind part."

"Just make sure they don't keep on going with your rusty red hair hangin' on their belt."

They decided against a fire, instead each taking a handful of jerked venison, and at late morning busied themselves saddling up. Again Sam waited and studied their back trail for a while as the others went on ahead. In the distance the Big Belt Mountains loomed over them, now white-capped, soon to be totally white.

Sam waited a half hour, then, seeing no trace of pursuers, gigged Blue into a lope and in another half hour had caught up with them. The women were astride, leading the two pack animals, and the old man was again afoot.

Dismounting, Sam walked along with Silas for a while, curious if there was more to the Indian encounter than just random fate. He'd remembered that old Silas had known one of the Indians and called him by name, Hunting Hawk.

His curiosity was piqued.

"Silas," he asked, "you knew that bunch?"

The old man glanced over at him, and his eyes darkened. "I know the blue-belly beggars."

"How so?"

"I lived a winter with Mrs. McGraw's people, the highcountry Blackfeet, many winters ago. A bunch of Cree had stripped my camp, kilt my son, and left me about the way you found me staked out last night. The Blackfeet and I had traded some, and they took me in and saved my bacon. I took a shine to Talking Woman, but had nothing to offer her daddy for her."

For a moment, Sam thought about asking about his son, then figured it would be better to let bad memories lie. "So how'd you end up with her?"

"Hunting Hawk was from a cousin tribe, the Bloods, from way down the Missouri near where the Yellowstone joins her, and he brought a dozen crow-bait horses. . . . Actually, that ain't right, they was fine horses, most stolen army mounts from one of the mapping gangs. And he carried her off after using them and some hides as the bride payment."

His attitude was still dark, as if it was all a bad memory he'd as soon forget.

"So, he's got her now. Then what?"

"Then I headed to the Missouri, worked my way down to Fort Benton, got myself a stake, including a fine Colt revolving rifle I later traded for this'n 'cause it had more kick, and headed out to get her back."

"And you did."

"I did, stole her right outta Hunting Hawk's camp, north of the Missouri, way out in the plains . . . along with a pair of fine horses. She went, kickin' an' screamin', but not so much as she convinced me that she truly had it in her heart that she wanted to stay. We rode hard with old Hunting Hawk and his band hot on our trail, all the way down to the Missouri where we lost the beggars in the breaks, then south to the Yellowstone, then up it all the way to the bubblin' mud country. After two hard seasons there, Mary came along, and there weren't no longer any question of Hunting Hawk."

"That must have been a couple of decades back."

"A long spell. Mary has eighteen summers."

"But old Hunting Hawk didn't forget?"

"He probably wants my scalp more'n a summer's worth o' prime hides. Yesterday was the third run-in we had with him over the years. I thought I had him dead to rights last night, when I rode back into their camp after getting a jump on them ol' boys, but the old man ain't so slow as he might be. He jumped like a goosed toad frog when he spied me acomin', and I think I missed . . . damn the flies. The som'bitch shot my dog, and I was partial to ol' dog."

"You think he'll be after us?"

"Sure as old buff chips burn."

"Maybe I ought to drop back for a while."

"Let's keep the oars in the water and plow forward for a good long spell. They's still got the whiskey-bottle blues, an' won't be working up a real mad till they wears off."

Had Charley Mad-in-the-Morning and Little Ears been so inclined, they would have winked at each other as Rusty Pacovsky explained to them — with a combination of Cree, English, and sign lan guage — their mission. Actually, they understood every word of English that most of the white eyes used . . . but they indulged him, and benefited themselves, by keeping quiet. Also, they considered him a little crazy, and that fact alone kept them paying close attention.

"The sheriff thinks ol' man McGraw will head west over the old trading trail, across the Big Belts. And he thinks this man Stranahan is ridin' along. We'll take the wagon road until we pass the Big Belts, then head north and try and pick them up when they drop down to cross the Missouri. With any luck, the snow in the Big Belts will slow 'em down." As he talked, he used sign language as best he could, which was not good at all. Both Indians merely stood with arms crossed in front of them, waiting for him to quit yapping so they could get on with the job at hand.

"If we get him, he goes to the Great Father, and we bring his carcass back here. You get vittles and five dollars each gold money, and a quart of corn whiskey for each of you, if we catch him. Understand?" Both Indians managed a single nod.

"Good," Pacovsky said. "I'll be at your camp at sunup. Be saddled up and each of you have an extra mount and vittles for at least three or four days. We got some hard ridin' ahead."

Again he got the nod; then he turned on his heel and headed for the President Madison. It would be a beefsteak and a bottle of whiskey for him, as they'd be a couple of days without either as they ran Stranahan to ground.

As he strode down Bozeman's mud street, he thought back on the events of the last week. His highfalutin brother had made the mistake of becoming a hero in the eyes of most Bozeman residents, when he'd shot down robbers on two occasions, riding shotgun on the Bozeman-Helena stage. So much of a hero that he'd announced that he was going to run against Sheriff Hiram Thacker in the upcoming election.

And the consensus was that it would be a landslide for Jud Pacovsky.

As popular as Jud Pacovsky had become, Thacker had become equally unpopular. In fact, most of Bozeman hated Thacker. It seemed that every supposed infraction of the law resulted in a healthy fine, and Thacker seemed to live better and better with every fine the city collected. He was also suspected of being in cahoots with a local merchant, Quinton Handley Weaver.

It seemed every time Weaver bought hides or trade goods or gold dust and paid in cash, the man who sold the goods would be arrested on a minor infraction and fined heavily. It was suspected that Weaver received a good portion of the fine in return.

Even though Rusty Pacovsky had been told by Sheriff Thacker not to harm anyone when he and his two hired henchmen held up the stage, he knew that the sheriff would hold no grudge should Jud Pacovsky, Bozeman's hero, be shot down in the process.

Jud should never have mouthed off that his first item of business, should he be elected, would be to fire Deputy Rusty Pacovsky, his worthless brother.

That had cost him dearly. Even a man with a scattergun full of dimes was no match for a bushwacker with a long rifle holed up behind a rock a hundred yards away — a bushwhacker from Kansas who could hit a dime with a Winchester at a hundred paces, and had proved it many times during the recent unpleasantries.

Pacovsky smiled as he climbed the steps of the President Madison. Hell, older brothers should know that their much younger brothers would grow up someday, and that someday there might be hell to pay.

The best of his coming trip was he'd get a chance at the half-breed daughter. Every time he'd seen her, she'd just kept getting riper and riper, and it was time she was picked.

And Rusty Pacovsky was just the Montana man to do the job.

Eight

When Liam Stranahan entered the Kaiser, he was surprised to see Gunter Kauffmann leaning against the bar. He figured Gunter would be up the trail, wanting to view the body before he paid up.

Gunter was laughing and chatting with a couple of other miners, and didn't see Liam approach.

"I'm going to set down to a plate, Kauffmann. Maybe you'd join me as we have business."

Gunter turned, saw his partner in apparent good health, and the blood drained from his face.

"Surprised to see me, Gunter?" Liam asked.

"I . . . Well, I . . ." the big German mumbled.

"Come to the table. Even a condemned man deserves a last good meal."

"What does that mean?" Gunter managed, recovering his composure.

"You should know." Liam walked to a table, out of earshot of the bar, and took a seat, never taking his eyes off Kauffmann, and sitting so his back was to the wall.

Gunter turned back to the bar long enough to pick up and down his drink, then looked back at Liam. The surprise was gone, and now he had fire in his eyes. He stomped over and jerked a chair out and settled in.

"So, you didn't go back to the mine last night?" Gunter stated the obvious.

"I was told the trail would be less than hospitable."

"And who tolt you that?"

"You were overheard, Kauffmann."

"What do you mean?"

"Overheard. Surely you understand that word, Gunter?"

"I understand perfectly, but it means nothing to me."

"You should have been in the theater, a thespian, Gunter. You're a good enough actor to have played right alongside John Wilkes Booth. . . . You've got the same interests as Booth. . . . Then again you don't have the looks for it."

"What the hell you talking about, Stranahan? Talk English."

Gunter was beginning to slip back into a heavy German accent, which Liam had noticed he did when he was tired or upset. This time Liam attributed it to pure anger, as Gunter's face was beginning to redden.

Liam, too, was beginning to fume, something he'd promised himself he wouldn't do. He rose slowly to his feet, one balled fist clinched at his side, his right palm resting on the butt of his revolver. "I am speaking English, Kauffmann. Now, are you going to sell out to me, or am I going to go to the marshal and have a talk with him about you hiring some back-shootin' snake to get rid of your partner?" Liam was loud enough that the bartender stopped wiping down a table, and he and the miners at the bar turned to stare.

Gunter glanced over his shoulder, then continued, his voice lower now. "Sit back down, Liam. Let's talk dis over like two civilized men."

"Civilized men don't hire some snake to do their dirty work."

Liam stared at him, hoping he'd reach for the gun at his side, but he didn't. Instead, he smiled. "Liam, sit down."

Finally, Liam relented, and retook his seat. The bartender walked over to the table before they could continue.

s was almost concluded, he would have
k look at the horse's shoes after all. As
did so, he noticed that the fire had
ned down to an ashen pile.

Erik!" he called out, as he dropped to
 ground. He still had a hand on the
n, and one on the horse's rump, when
gruff German voice rang out.

Just keep your hands up, Irishman."

lowly, without lowering his hands from
horse's back, he glanced back over his
ulder. Gunter stood in an open stall
r, a double-barrel shotgun in hand, its
zzles pointed directly at Liam's mid-
ion.

Where's Erik?" Liam asked.

You stupid Irish. Erik always takes his
ch wid his woman. He's blocks away."

Decide to do your own dirty work,
nter?"

If you vant something done right, do it
elf is something you always said,
hman."

iam slowly turned, his hands still
ed, but now at shoulder height. As he
ared away with the big German, he
ced at the back of the barn.

Erik, glad you're back," he called out.

unter couldn't help himself, and
ced at the doors at the rear of the

"You fellows want to order some chow?"

"I do," Liam said. "Steak and over-easy eggs."

"Got pork chops, no steak today."

"Then pork chops, and coffee. Lots of black coffee. Black as old Gunter's heart."

"You, sir?" he turned to Gunter.

"No, thanks," Gunter managed, turning his attention immediately back to Liam.

"You off your feed, Gunter? Never saw you turn down a chance to put your trotters up to the trough. Guess you figure eatin' pork would be a little on the cannibalistic side."

"Vat you talkin' about? You still vant to buy my share?"

"It's a standing offer."

"You said a thousand last time we talk."

"That was before you hired a dog to gun me down."

Gunter hesitated for a long moment, and Liam let him stew.

"Den how much you offer?"

"Five hundred. It's what your half of that worthless pile of crap is worth."

Gunter began to redden again, but he hesitated answering and glanced around the room before he continued. The bartender was in the back and the two miners had gone back to drinking and talking.

Finally, he centered his hard eyes on Liam.

"I will take five hundred, and you won't be having any talks wit the marshal."

"Done. I'd shake on it, Gunter, but I don't want to get my hands dirty." Gunter's jaw knotted, but he said nothing. "You don't go back to the mine. I'll box up your things and leave them for you at the livery the next time I'm down. Erik Vandermer's place."

"You got the money?" Gunter asked.

"I'll go to the bank right now. I'll have them draw up a paper . . . a bill of sale. You going to wait here?"

"I have udder business. You bring it to Vandermer's at twelve-thirty. I am going to have him shoe my horse . . . takin' my money and headin' back to Helena."

"I'll be ready before then."

"Twelve-thirty, if you vant to buy me out."

Liam shrugged. "I'll see you there, now leave me to eat so my stomach don't turn at the sight of you."

Gunter got up and stomped away, but he had a tight smile on his face that Liam couldn't see.

After Liam had finished, and calmed down, he went to the bank and withdrew five hundred dollars in scrip, and had Wil-

liam Smithson, the banker, dra[w] of sale for half interest in the Si[x] and Two. He realized he shoul[d] Gunter come with him to th[e] Smithson could witness his m[a] was too late. Vandermer could would surely have a pen and we[ll] Gunter could sign.

Liam still had time to kill, so h[e] in at the Phillipsburg Merca[ntile] browsed. He came to some bolt[s] and admired a kelly-green satin. *would look fine on Maureen O[* thought. *I'll just have to bring her and buy her some of that, and take millinery shop. We're going to have to celebrate.* He smiled at the thou[ght]

Spending over thirty minutes about the store, he finally bough[t] some hard candy and a *Leslie's* [*] was only a month old, and would reading, now that he wouldn't [be] company up at the mine.

Finally, glancing at his watch, h[e] the livery.

When he got there, he gigged th[e] skin through the double doors a[nd] seeing Kauffmann about, disn[...] where he could tie up near the bell[...] ciding that since he was here, and h[e]

barn, instantly recognizing Liam's ploy.

Liam grabbed for the revolver at his side, managing to clear the holster, cocking it as it came up . . . but he wasn't quite fast enough.

Both barrels of the twelve-gauge scatter-gun exploded, blowing Liam back against his horse, but not until he'd gotten off a premature shot. The buckskin, taking a few stray pellets, bolted, spun, and retreated out the front doors of the livery, making Liam spiral onto the hay-covered floor. He convulsed a few times, a huge hole venting his chest, then lay still.

Dust settled from the barn's rafters, as Liam bled out the last of his life's fluids.

Gunter, grasping his side, blood seeping between his fingers, stumbled forward and stooped, going through Liam's pockets until he found the deed, and the money.

He managed to gather enough strength to kick Liam squarely in the ribs, hard enough to half roll him over, then he made his way to the rear doors of the barn, and disappeared.

Nine

They'd traveled north a while after crossing the Shields and up into the low hills, until they picked up the headwaters of Deep Creek, then turned west again toward a deep cut in the Big Belt Mountains.

Sam noticed some small piles of rocks by the trail. He had noticed them before, and yelled up to Silas, "What are these stacks of stones?"

"Them are guideposts along the trading trail, but more than that, they are the red man's way of giving thanks for a safe journey. New travelers place a stone, and before long, it's a clear sign that this is a good trail, a good way to go, a good part of life."

"Well, hell, Silas, you're afoot. Stack a stone up there for us. So far we've been well watched over."

"Don't mind if'n I do," Silas said, and paused to add a flat stone to the three-foot-high symbol. Both of the women had reined up, and watched. They nodded in seeming agreement, then reined away again.

It had clouded up some, and heavy billowy clouds with great crowns like piles of cotton on a flat table threatened their coming. Sam could see streaks of rain, or maybe snow, under the dark flat bottoms of the imposing clouds ahead, and by the time they reached the toe of the mountains, it was misting heavily, with all signs of direct sun only a fond memory.

Sam pulled his wide-brimmed hat tighter, then the buff robe from behind his saddle and wrapped it around his shoulders.

Silas dropped back to walk beside Blue for a moment.

"I'll have Mary make you a tie for that soon as we camp."

"That would be fine, Silas. We in for some hard weather?"

"Trail stays pretty low, but it's gettin' time for a good blow. Maybe it'll discourage ol' Huntin' Hawk from doggin' our trail."

"You think he'd chase us this far?"

"That ol' coon'll track us clear to Helena if he thinks he can get a hank o' my hair.

He won't like coming into Deep Creek Canyon, as there's been plenty of folks come and go here over the years. Most of them mud-ruckin' miners. I sent the army after ol' Hunting Hawk once, but he's slippery as a salamander."

"Maybe I ought to lay back again?"

"Give it another day; then we can start to fret."

That night they camped in the dead silence of a heavy snowfall, alongside Deep Creek. They had already passed the sign of miners, who had worked Deep Creek over the years. Silas told Sam about Confederate Gulch, to the north, which had proven to be one of the richest placer deposits ever found. Diamond City was still filled with miners and merchants. The occasional small pile of tailings marked the creek, and a few scars in the mountainside showed where the more hardworking had plied the hard rock for veins.

They made supper of the last of the bacon and beans, as most of their supplies had been left behind in the Blood camp. If they didn't get lucky with the wildlife, their stomachs would be sticking to their backbones by nightfall.

The flakes fell big as aspen leafs, and by the time they awoke, everything was covered in three inches of fluffy powder. But the snow had stopped, and the sun, rimmed with a ring of yellow, was trying to fight its way through the cloud cover to regain control.

The last of their coffee was brewed and boiling stronger by the time Sam had saddled up, and he took the time to drink his share. Then he again used his buff bedroll for a wrap, only this time he didn't have to hold it in place, as Mary had fashioned a rawhide tie by the light of last night's campfire.

While the others broke camp, Sam rode back a half mile to a high spot so he could see their back trail. As he sat studying, the eerie echo of a bugling bull elk rang up from somewhere below near the creek, and was promptly answered by another bull somewhere above him. *I am the king of these mountains,* the first said, and the other replied, *Prove it.* There was no sound in the mountains that so exemplified pagan wildness as did the bugle of a rutting bull elk. Had one not heard it before, he would think fire-breathing hounds of hell were on his trail.

Slowly edging back, Sam worked his way down to where he'd tied the grulla to an aspen, slipped the Winchester out of its saddle scabbard, then made his way back up to his hidey-hole.

He again studied their back trail, as it wouldn't do to signal any pursuer as to where they were, but with the snow, a blind man could now follow their trail. Besides, the heavy air would muffle the sound of a shot.

He waited, listening as the bulls continued to challenge each other, until the higher bull came into sight two hundred or more yards across the draw. He was a monarch, with at least seven points on each side.

The big bull paused on the ridge across from where Sam waited, laid his antlers back, and stretched his neck, screaming at the affront of the younger bull, who had the audacity to be in his territory, then tore up the patch of grass beneath his hooves, and rattled the underbrush demonstrating his anger with his massive antlers. His breath roiled in the cold, and mist lifted off the heat of his back. Again he bugled, and again he was answered by the other bull, even closer to where Sam patiently still-hunted.

Crashing timber whetted Sam's anticipation. A smaller bull charged out of a grove of river willows below, and into a clearing less than one hundred yards from Sam.

Carefully he sighted on the bull's vitals below the deep dark coat on neck, shoulders, and chest, much heavier than that on his hindquarters. The bull laid his antlers back along his spine, and, stiff-legged, sounded another challenge. He was a much smaller four-by-five, and Sam figured he would be a little more tender eating than the old monarch. Besides, he was in range.

He squeezed the trigger, just as the sights touched behind the front shoulder and low in the chest, so he would get the heart as well as lungs. The first shot echoed down the draw, but the bull didn't even flinch, intent on the threat to his cows from the bull above.

Damn, I couldn't have missed, Sam chastised himself as he levered in another shell.

He fired again, and this time the bull turned, his eyes flaring, and looked at him, then spun and charged back into the willows.

Could I have banged this sight against something? he wondered, studying both the front sight and the rear one on the receiver. Both seemed just fine. But appearances could deceive, particularly when it came to the fickle sights of a rifle.

He took his time making his way back to Blue, mounted, and reined around the little ridge until he found the spot in the clearing where the bull had stopped. More than pleased, he spotted a small dab of pink frothy lung blood.

Having shot many an elk in the Judith country, he was not overly surprised that the animal had shown no sign of being hit. He'd come to respect how incredibly tough the elk were. Even if he hit this one twice in the vitals, he could have a long search to find him.

But he was blessed by a God who didn't want them to go hungry, and found the critter after a short two hundred yards, in the bottom of the ravine, half in and half out of Deep Creek. Both shots had been right on target, within two inches of each other, and both should have hit the heart.

Roping the animal's antlers, he gigged the grulla and with great effort on the horse's part, dragged the eight-hundred-pound creature clear of the creek, then dismounted and went to work gutting him.

It would be elk heart and liver for dinner. And as cold as it was, the fresh meat would last them until they got to Helena. They wouldn't even have to take time to jerk some.

He had barely gotten the animal gutted when Silas showed up, mounted on one packhorse, and leading the other.

"Thought you might have been scalped and roasted by now," Silas said with a wry smile. "Then again, thought you might have a little whitetail down in this here creek bed. But this here is a treat." He dismounted, dragging a knife from a scabbard on his belt, and went to work. "Still and all, let's put the hurry-up on it. If I know my heathens, old Hunting Hawk won't be far behind."

"Get a handful of hide, old man, and let's get back to the ladies and have our feet by the fire in Helena before we get caught up."

"You done got the intestines all dirty. The women will be spittin' mad we don't bring 'em back some to roast."

Sam shook his head, guessing he still had some things to learn.

"We gonna save this hide?" Sam asked.

"It's your kill," Silas answered, then looked a little mischievous. "But you might want to give hide and horn to one of the women . . . whichever one you'd favor with a gift."

"Which is valued the most?"

"Hide."

In an hour the animal was skinned, boned, and packed in the panniers, and they headed back downstream.

With luck and a day and a half's hard riding, or maybe two, they should be worrying about where to ford the Missouri. Then another two days, they should be in Helena, enjoying Liam's hospitality.

God willing and the creek don't rise, thought Sam, *and the damn Bloods and the law stay far behind, and the weather stays at least somewhat tolerable.*

Seems like a lot to ask.

Gunter managed to get the bleeding in his side stopped before he reached the mine. The shot had gone clean through, and, he guessed, since he was still alive, hadn't hit any vitals. When he reined up to the small corral, across a clearing from the little cabin he and Liam had shared, Tucker Stark stepped out of the log structure.

"Didn't never see yer pard. Thought I'd come on up here and make myself to home and maybe he'd come along."

Gunter glared at the tall gaunt man, lean as a rattlesnake, who'd gained some reputation as a gunfighter. The man's black hair was slicked back, and his dark eyes deep-set and somewhat foreboding. "I took care of it myself. Don't need you now."

"You shot him down?" Tucker smiled, his lips taut on his sallow face.

"I did. He's dead as a roasted cock."

"Looks like he shot back," Tucker eyed Gunter's bloody side. "Well, I guess I'm only entitled to part of my fee."

"Part, hell. You got more'n vat you deserve wit the twenty-dollar deposit."

The tall man strode purposefully across the clearing until he was face-to-face with Gunter. "I laid up in the cold on that damned trail half the night. Weren't my fault the bloody Irishman didn't show up like you said he would. . . . That was sure 'nuff your fault."

Stark stood, glaring, slightly leaning forward, resting his hand on the pearl handle of the heavy revolver.

"I vill pay you another twenty dollars in gold."

"Make it thirty; then I'll have half of what would have been coming to me, had he shown."

Gunter sighed deeply. "Twenty-five."

"The hell you say. I was supposed to get a fine buckskin horse and his gear as well."

"All right, all right. Another thirty."

The hand dropped away from the pearl

grip, and a tight smile again crossed the sallow face.

"You vill be riding out of the country, if I pay you?"

"Hell, there ain't nothing to keep me around here."

Gunter dug in his pocket and pulled out his purse, careful to make sure the gunman couldn't see in it as he retrieved a ten- and a twenty-dollar gold piece.

He handed them over.

"Obliged," Tucker said, and tipped his hat.

He started back toward the house, then stopped. "That's a fine scattergun you got tied on that saddle. I'd be further obliged if'n you walked along with me to retrieve my horse from 'round back of the house."

"I got to go lie down, before I bleed to death —"

"Not more important than me not getting shot in the back with a load of buckshot. Walk along with me, Gunter. And leave the shotgun where it rests."

"Humph," Gunter managed, but did as requested. The fact was, shooting the man, the only real witness to his crime, had crossed his mind.

As he watched the tall man ride away from the mine, he was glad to be rid of him, almost as glad as he was to be rid of Liam Stranahan.

Betsylou Maddigan and Maureen "Helen" O'Toole stood staring down at the peaceful face of Liam Stranahan. The barber who doubled as the undertaker had been thoughtful enough to cover the body with a blanket, sparing them from viewing the terrible wound in his chest.

Tears rolled down Maureen's cheeks, and she began to sob. Then she gathered herself together. "He was a fine man and I loved him, and could have loved him with all my heart. Only today, he said he was going to change my name."

"Some of us was meant to be heartbroken, lass. You and I seem to be hexed when it comes to men."

Marshal Clark Peckham, his vest adorned with his copper badge, walked into the rear of the barbershop, which doubled as an undertaker's parlor.

"Ladies, I need to have a word with you."

The words flowed out of Betsylou like a flood. In a very few minutes, the marshal was convinced he had a good suspect in Gunter Kauffmann.

As he was returning to his office, he was

greeted on the street by Parker Willingham, the postmaster and express company
stationmaster.

"Marshal Peckham, I got a copy of a will
here that you'd better have a look at."

"Will?"

"Liam Stranahan, he came by my office
and wrote out a last will and testament in
his own hand. I witnessed it and kept the
only copy in my safe, at his request."

"Now that's interesting —"

"Not half so interesting as who he left as
one of the beneficiaries."

"And who would that be?"

"Well, there was only two. A Samuel
Stranahan, who Liam said was his brother,
and our own Miss Helen, legally known, or
so Liam said, as Maureen O'Toole. Ain't
that a hoot? She must work that little lady
thing like a mare munchin' oats."

The marshal frowned at Willingham,
surprised that the little man would come
up with such a thing, then scratched his
head as Willingham adjusted his glasses
and blushed slightly.

"Well, that is interesting. More than just a
little interesting, as I was about to ride up
the mountain to find out if Liam Stranahan
was related to Sam. I got a wanted handbill
on Sam. Came in on yesterday's stage."

"That is interesting?" Willingham said with a guffaw. "If that mine proves to be worth a hoot, we could be losing us a soiled dove. She'll be wearing silk and satin and living up on the hill with the respectable folks."

"Doubt that, but there's more than one way to lose a soiled dove, Parker. Looks like she's got as good a motive to shoot old Liam down as does his partner. We could lose her permanent to the rope."

"You don't think —"

"I don't jump to any conclusions, Parker. That's part of being a good marshal.

"I never woulda guessed."

"That's why you are no marshal. I guess I'd better have a little more of a talk with Miss Helen, or whatever the hell her name is. Then tomorrow, should Miss Helen not confess, I'll be riding up to have a little chat with Gunter Kauffmann."

"He'll probably be down tomorrow . . . for Liam's funeral."

"I doubt it, knowing how much bad blood there seemed to be between them. If he's coming, I'll meet him on the trail and ride back down with him."

Ten

When Sam and Silas returned to their camp, the ladies had things ready to load on the packhorses. They both smiled and laughed in relief when Silas told them what the packs contained. To add to their joy, the weather was beginning to break; any sign of snow had passed, and in fact the three inches they'd received was beginning to melt off. If the sun truly broke through, the melt-off would begin in earnest.

Talking Woman wanted to stay and roast the intestines right there, but Silas insisted they pack up and ride at least until early afternoon, when they could pick another campsite. By that time they should be within sight, or only an hour or so, from the Missouri River Valley, somewhere above the steep cliffs cut by the Missouri that Lewis and Clark had named the Gates of the Mountains. They had enough venison jerky to last them the rest of the day, and while Silas had been gone to see what the shooting was about, the women had managed to fill a small gathering bag with the remnants of some fall berries. Reluctantly, she relented, when reminded that Hunting Hawk and the Bloods might be close behind.

The packhorses were each well burdened with over two hundred pounds of meat, hide, and horns, so the three riders each tied an additional bundle on the back of their horses. But they now would be well fed for the rest of the trip.

Deep Creek Canyon was unusual, as the creek gathered in the Shields River Valley — in a drainage separate from the river that flowed north — and flowed westward, traversing the Big Belt Range via a deep twenty-mile-long cut, directly across the range. The canyon crossed the range as if a woman had taken a pie knife and cut a wedge out of, and perpendicular to, the range. The mountains, hard and granite-shouldered on the ridges above, climbed steeply from the creek bed, and the creek continued to grow, nourished by pine- and fir-lined feeder creeks that tumbled out of the high mountains on either side.

After they'd ridden for half a day, Sam gigged Blue up alongside where Silas strode behind the two women with his heavy pack. "You think I might ought to ride up to that ridge and take a gander behind us?"

"Wouldn't fret me if'n you did, ol' coon. We took a lot of time with that big critter."

"Would old Hunting Hawk be stupid enough to ride into a canyon like this, knowing his enemy might have the high ground?"

Silas paused a moment, and lowered his pack for a rest as the women rode on. "Hunting Hawk is big medicine with his people. He's got a bit of a pot on him now, but he was built like a man mountain . . . still is . . . and was always undefeated in battle. In fact the old boy has never been touched by the bullet of white man or Indian. When he was young, some time before the time he came to fetch Talking Woman, he went on a vision quest. The great bear told him that if he brought him one of his wives, he would gain the bear's power."

"For giving up one of his wives?"

"No, not just for giving one up, but for sacrificing one. He did. He brought the youngest of his three wives, killed her on the mountaintop where he'd got the vision, and covered her with rocks. Later it was

124

said a big ol' griz dug her up and et her.

"Since that time, all Indians and most white men have feared the old boy. He thinks he's invincible and can't be touched by man or lead. And he's killed plenty of them to prove it. He's hell on wheels when he's full of whiskey, and has killed more than a dozen of his own people when he's whiskey-soaked, and no tellin' how many whites. I always had the hunch ol' Three Leg Wolf, Talking Woman's daddy, was right happy I'd stolt her away."

"And what do you think of this 'power'?"

"Hell, I ain't never been able to crease his ugly hide. But then again, he never shot one of my own, and now he done went and shot ol' dog. If'n ol' Hawk can be shot, them I'm up to doin' the job."

Sam scratched his head under the wide-brimmed hat, then shook his head in wonder. "Well, let's hope he's gettin' old and tired. So old he's hardly in need of a woman."

"I wouldn't count on it, ol' coon. He ain't much older than this young stud horse." Silas patted himself on the chest, drawing a smile from Sam.

As Silas readjusted the pack and hurried to catch up with the ladies, Sam reined the grulla through a patch of river willow, then climbed some soft earth under a few lodgepole pines. Then the slope rose even more steeply, and the horse really had to work to climb a steep grade of scree. It was three strides forward and two back as the horse clawed up the steep slope, until finally Sam dismounted and, himself on all fours most of the time, led the animal. After a hard scramble they topped the ridge, two hundred feet above the creek bottom.

He dropped Blue's reins to let the big horse graze on the sparse grass of the ridge top, and took a seat on an outcropping to watch his back trail. A pair of golden eagles cavorted high overhead, catching the updrafts of the new warmth hitting the slopes below, then engaging each other in some mating ritual, and free-falling almost back to earth, only to climb again and repeat the entanglement.

Three or four hundred yards above where he rested, a dozen mule deer pawed at the slopes, exposing grass. Below him, surveying the widening creek, an osprey glided, then dove to snatch a small fish. He flew away to some perch where he could eat in peace, readjusting the fish so it faced the direction he flew, and wouldn't impede his flight.

Sam took a moment to drink in the beauty of the Big Belts. High above him, well above the muleys, separated by a slash of aspens still golden in the morning light, a herd of Rocky Mountain bighorn sheep leaped from rock to rock traversing a cliff side where even a cougar couldn't follow.

He had a pack full of food, some fine friends — one of whom was a beautiful woman — a good horse, some dependable weapons, and it looked like the sun was going to soon bless them with its warmth. What more could a man ask for?

Then he suddenly realized what more. In the distance, maybe a mile and a half up the creek the way they'd come, riders traversed a clearing.

Damn the luck. Was it the Indian who couldn't be touched by bullet or blade? The dozen Blood braves who wanted old Silas's hide to adorn their camp?

Although Sam couldn't make out who they were at that distance, he had to presume it was Hunting Hawk on their trail.

He recovered Blue, mounted, put the spurs to him, and hung on for dear life as the big stud set his front legs, hunkered down on his rear, and took the steep slope. They made it safely to the bottom, to Sam's great surprise, then galloped through the lodgepole pines and the river willows and picked up the trail.

The McGraws were only a half mile ahead of him, and he caught up quickly.

He slid the horse to a halt. "Silas, there's riders not two miles behind us."

"Cache the packs and dump your loads. We can always come back and fetch them. Better than slow horses and losing our scalps."

In moments, Silas and the women had stowed the panniers in the nearby brush. The women took up a trot, Silas mounted one of the packhorses and followed, while Sam took up the rear.

There was nowhere to go but straight down the canyon as the walls were so steep. And no matter where they went, they would be easily followed, as there was still enough snow on the ground that their trail could be followed at a gallop.

Rusty Pacovsky and the two Cree had made good time; in a couple of miles they would be turning north away from the Gallatin River and following Blacktail Creek north, then over a low divide to the Missouri Valley. In two days of hard riding they would reach the old Indian trading trail, they hoped before the McGraws made it out of the Big Belts. If they actually were headed that way.

By trading off their mounts, as each man led a second horse, and by carrying little in the way of supplies, they could make thirty miles a day.

With luck, they would be cozied up by a warm fire looking down on the trail with a clear field of fire long before old man McGraw and Stranahan came along. And of course, the tender morsel, Mary. Rusty had made clear to Little Ears and Charley Mad-in-the-Morning that the woman was his. As long as they stayed sober, there would be no problem. Which was a problem, as Rusty couldn't help bringing along a quart of rye, which he had hidden in his bedroll. But the Indians wouldn't know it was there, and he'd only take a draw on it should it turn bone-soakin' cold.

The best of it was the fact that the express company had added a good chunk to the reward. Rusty's half would be two hundred fifty dollars. Hell, that was damn nigh four months' wages.

Ol' Stranahan was gold on the hoof. Even though both he and Sheriff Thacker knew he was innocent.

And Rusty meant to reap the reward.

Not only for the money, but to pay back the scum for the slap. Rusty's lip was still swollen.

He'd bring him back dead, which would be a hell of a lot less trouble.

They camped that night on a pass overlooking the Missouri far below. By late the next afternoon they would be at the Indian trail. Things were going very well. Just at dusk, a snowshoe rabbit had bolted from under Little Ears's path, and he'd killed it on a dead run with one shot from the Golden Boy he carried. They roasted it and had hard biscuits. Rusty managed to unroll his bedroll without the Cree seeing the bottle of whiskey, and slipped it under his saddle, which he used for a backrest.

As much as he wanted a long draw on the bottle, he'd wait until business was done.

The soiled dove Helen had been summoned to Marshal Clark Peckham's small office. The marshal had spent a good part of the early afternoon interviewing the townspeople to find out what they knew about Stranahan's murder, and he'd come up with some interesting information. Now he wanted to get it from the mouth of one who he believed might have been the murderess, or at the least, an accomplice.

He rose as she walked in, dressed like a fine city lady. Had any single man not known her profession, he would be more than merely tempted to spark her. When she had come to Phillipsburg she'd been as plain as a house sparrow and as shy as a field mouse. Miss Betsylou had made the young woman bloom into a rose, even if into one with a certain kind of societal thorn that poisoned her for any decent man. She had her auburn hair in a bun and wore a yellow bonnet that matched both her lace-trimmed dress and parasol. Her cheeks were rouged and her mouth reddened by some concoction women used, but it was the emerald eyes, flawless complexion, and hair the hue of polished rosewood that set her apart from all the other women in Phillipsburg. Not that there were many.

"Have a seat, Miss Helen," Peckham said, rising as she entered.

"Thank you," she said, sitting primly in a seat across the desk from the marshal, her hands folded demurely in her lap. "I've told you all I know about Liam's last hours, Marshal. So may I ask what this is about?"

"How about a cup of coffee?"

131

"No, thank you. I have to get back to Miss Betsylou's. We have chores, you know."

"I'd suppose."

He let her stew while he rose, went to the potbellied stove, picked up the pot, warmed his cup, then returned to his seat.

Clark leaned forward and folded his hands on his desk. "Looks like you've become a woman of property."

"Pardon me?"

"Parker Williamson hasn't contacted you?"

"No. Why would Parker Williamson contact me?" she said, then blushed slightly, for her profession was one that the contact by most men wouldn't be surprising.

"The will. Liam Stranahan's last will and testament."

Helen sat in stunned silence for a moment.

So the marshal continued, "Helen is a made-up name, isn't it?"

She was silent for a moment, then nodded.

"And what would your real name be?"

"I was born an O'Toole of the O'Tooles of county Cork in the Emerald Isle. My given name is Maureen."

"Then it's definitely you who's named in Liam's will."

She began to cry, and Peckham had to strengthen his resolve. Either she was truly heartbroken, or was one of the great actresses of the time.

"Don't be bawling, Miss Helen, er . . . Miss Maureen. I can't stand it when a woman bawls."

She collected herself and dug a hankie out of the small lace bag that hung from her wrist, dabbing her eyes.

"I didn't want . . . or expect . . . anything from Liam. I just wish he were here. I just hope you're going after that partner of his."

"Well, you got something. You got one half of Liam's half interest in the Siglinda One and Two. It's been making a fair living for Liam and Gunter, and could make a lot more . . . at least Liam thought it might."

"I would never have guessed."

"He never let on?"

"No. I knew he thought highly of me. . . . In fact . . ."

"In fact what?"

"I had high hopes that he wanted to take me away from Miss Betsylou's." She again blushed.

Peckham was quiet for a moment, then

133

said, "Well, it's obvious he thought pretty highly of you." They sat in silence for a moment. "And it's obvious to me that you and Miss Betsylou think Gunter gunned him down."

"With good reason."

Peckham's look hardened. "Then why did you entertain Gunter up in your room last night, before Liam arrived?"

This time she blushed deeply, looking out the window for a moment. She again dabbed at her eyes. Then she centered them on Peckham and he could see sparks in the emerald. "That's what I'm paid for, Mr. Peckham, as if you didn't know. Gunter Kauffmann was a lout and a ruffian, and I hated spending even a second with the man, but I'm expected to . . . to entertain any man who has the price of a token. That won't happen again. In fact it would suit me fine if I could poison the whiskey he seems to like so well."

"You mean that?"

"It would be tempting."

"So, didn't you and Gunter make some kind of agreement? Gunter didn't want Liam as a partner. He made that clear in a couple of arguments that were overheard by townspeople. I think you shot Liam down in order to get half his interest in the mine, or you had Gunter shoot him down, and have offered to sell Gunter your interest when the deed was done."

Eleven

Miss Helen rose slowly, glaring at the marshal. "I loved Liam, and would never have harmed him in any way. I hate Gunter Kauffmann, and hope he rots in hell for what he's done."

"Maybe you would poison him, just to shut him up."

"I might like to poison him, but I wouldn't. I'm going to count on you to do your job . . . to bring him to justice."

"I don't know that he's done anything. I only have the word of a pair of whores that something was heard, and they don't even know who said it, and who, for sure, it was said to."

She stomped to the door, then paused and glanced back. "Betsylou may be a lot of things but a liar isn't one of them, nor am I. Gunter Kauffmann should be in one of those cells back there. Then, after he's given a fair trial, he should hang by his neck until he's as dead as Liam." She glared at him and the emerald eyes went icy. "Marshal Clark, don't you bother me again until that's a fact."

"The fact is, Miss Helen, you could find yourself in one of those cells." But she didn't hear the end of it, as she slammed the door behind her.

Clark Peckham rose. His coffee had gone cold again. He hated talking to a woman like that, but it was his job, and he meant to do it. Then again, it was easier talking to a whore and probable murderess, even if she was a beautiful woman.

Whoever had shot Liam Stranahan down would hang from a new pine gallows, woman or not.

Sam and the McGraws had ridden hard, trying to outdistance the band of Bloods. They'd made more than ten miles, most of it at a lope, and the horses were well winded. Finally, Talking Woman reined up. "My horse very tired. Afraid I kill him."

"Rest and water them," Sam said. "There's a pretty good lookout a couple of hundred yards back. I'll see if they're still doggin' us and —"

"They're still hot on our trail," Silas said, with no seeming doubt.

"And if so, how far," Sam continued as he reined the big grulla stud around.

In consideration of the animal, who wasn't nearly as winded as the McGraws' ponies, but was well lathered and breathing hard, Sam dropped his lead rope and let him graze as he climbed a brush-covered draw to work his way to a ridge over a hundred feet above the creek.

He only stayed on the ridge for a heartbeat, seeing the Indian band less than a half mile behind.

He scrambled down the slope, sliding on his butt part of the way, running the rest. Without the stirrup he swung into the saddle, and loped the roan back to where the McGraws waited. "They're close. I think we ought to fort up."

Silas cogitated a moment. "They's a small crick not far up ahead, if my old head serves me —"

"I remember," Talking Woman said.

"And a fifty-foot waterfall with a pool above and a wee meadow around it. It's a big ol' kinda hole in the mountain. They's a bit of a cave where we can hide the horses, and some feed. We can get there on horseback, and have a good shootin' look at any who try to follow. It's hard rock, and with luck they won't catch our track."

"Let's get there," Sam said, as the big stud danced impatiently behind the others.

They went at a full gallop, kicking snow and mud up behind them. After only a couple of hundred yards, Mary's horse stumbled, a forefoot in a hole, and rolled head over heels. Mary flew off, but somersaulted in the soft mud and snow and seemed to be unhurt, as she was almost as quickly on her feet. Sam reached down and swung her up behind him. They galloped on, with Mary's paint limping behind. It was a half mile to the creek the McGraws had remembered, but it was there. It was only a four-foot trickle working its way out of the willows lining the now thirty-foot-wide Deep Creek.

They rode directly in the stream, trying to hide their trail, then dismounted near the waterfall. Leading their horses, Mary's paint still limping behind, they made their way up a narrow game trail away from the waterfall. The granite cliff was almost vertical above them. Then it doubled back, and they soon found themselves entering the meadow, still spotted with snow, just above the waterfall. A forty-foot circular pool lay in the center of a snow-covered meadow twenty-five yards wide and almost forty yards long. A place you wouldn't have found unless you were determined to follow the creek up the mountain — a scooped-out place in a mountain of vertical walls above Deep Creek. Another waterfall, this one over a hundred feet high, fed the meadow pool from high above. The meadow was surrounded on three sides by almost sheer granite walls. A lot of driftwood had washed into the meadow from above and would serve as firewood. There was enough graze in sunny patches to keep the horses for three or four days.

It was as good a place as any to make a stand.

While the women herded the horses into the cave under the higher waterfall, Silas and Sam made ready for a fight.

They each found good hideouts near the topside of where the lower waterfall fell away, both with good views of Deep Creek below. The creek made a slow turn to the south in the canyon below, and they were stationed in the bottom of the curve, with good views of not only the creek below, but the walls on both sides, up and downstream from where they forted their standoff spots with whatever loose rock they could find.

Then, they waited.

As soon as he'd finished his conversation

with the soiled dove, Marshal Clark Peckham decided there was no reason to wait to talk with Gunter Kauffmann until he returned to Phillipsburg. He knew Kauffmann had left town that morning, some time after he'd had his argument with Liam, and he knew that Liam had gone to the bank for money and to have a deed and bill of sale drawn conveying a half interest in the claim from Kauffmann to him. But he didn't know if Liam was to meet with Kauffmann in town, or back at the mine. If they were to meet at Erik's Livery, then that put Kauffmann at the scene. But no one saw him there, even though some folks on the street had heard the shot. He had to presume the man was headed back to the mine. It was only six or seven roadless miles up to the mine, but the trail was a hard climb for a horse and would take the better part of three hours.

He was only an hour out of town, just after the trail narrowed and became steep, when he came face-to-face with another rider. And he didn't know the man, but he rode a fine-looking dappled gray.

"Howdy. Where you bound from?" the marshal asked.

The other man casually hooked a leg up over the horn, and fished the makin's out

141

of a shirt pocket while he considered the question.

"From up in the hills," he finally replied. He licked the cigarette paper and stuck the finished product between narrow lips, while he dug for a sulfur head. "Is it that there badge asking, or are you just being neighborly?"

"I'm heading up the trail on business, friend. You haven't been at the Siglinda mine, now, have you?"

"Again, is it the badge askin'?"

Peckham didn't like the man's manner, and sure didn't like his looks. The heavy revolver at his side was slung a little low, and the flat-brimmed hat was surely no Montana rig.

"Could be," Peckham said. "The Siglinda?"

"Never heard of the place. Been makin' my way over these mountains behind."

"Sure travel light for a fella's been in the high country."

"I got a tough hide, a place to go, and no money for googaws." The man gave him a tight smile, then dropped his leg from the saddle horn and gigged the horse.

"Be seein' you," he said, as he reined around on the high side of the lawman.

Peckham's animal sidestepped in the

narrow trail, his forefoot slipping off the side. He had to scramble to keep from heading down the steep mountainside, but managed to recover and regain the trail.

Peckham ungritted his teeth and called after the man, "And just where are you headed?"

"Hear'd there was a town called Phillipsburg up ahead a piece." He waved over his shoulder without looking back.

Marshal Peckham again gritted his teeth, and spurred the horse on up the trail. He had business ahead, and little time for drifters, no matter how fishy their story sounded.

It was the middle of the afternoon before he reined up at the Siglinda's little corral. He tied his horse and loosened the latigo.

To call the spot a mine was a bit of an exaggeration. Stranahan and Kauffmann had panned the stream for some time, taking a fair share of placer gold, but when they got bored, and the work became less productive, they'd started a hard-rock hole fifty feet above the creek bed into the side of the mountain where a number of quartz veins were exposed. Some of the veins had infinitesimal grains of gold showing, but not nearly enough to warrant crushing.

But who knew what might be deeper in the mountain? The placer gold flecking the creek had to come from somewhere.

Peckham yelled out to Kauffmann, half expecting the man to show his head from the mine up above, where the tailings showed that they hadn't dug any distance to speak of, but it was from the little cabin that Kaufmann answered, sticking only his upper body out and around the door, just far enough that Peckham could see he was dressed.

"Marshal. I be just a minute."

He disappeared back into the shack and in a minute or so, reappeared. Peckham couldn't help noticing that Kaufmann had changed shirts. The new one he'd put on was well soiled, so it wasn't vanity that made him change. And he had a gun strapped on his waist.

"Vat brings you to the Siglinda?" Gunter asked, a wide smile on his face.

"Bad news, Gunter, but then you already knew."

"Vat bad news?" His look hardened.

"Liam."

"So, vat's wit Liam?"

"Maybe you ought to tell me."

"Don't play games with me, Marshal. Vat's the problem wit my partner?"

"You going to invite me in?" Peckham asked.

"Place is a mess. Vat's the problem wit Stranahan?"

"Killed."

"Vat?" Kauffmann looked sincerely surprised.

"Shot down around noon in Erik Vandermer's place . . . not long after you left the Kaiser."

Kauffmann seemed to take a deep breath and settle down. Even his English got better. "What do you mean by that?"

"I mean, not long after you left the Kaiser, Liam was shot down. Just where did you go when you left?"

"Liam and I were not on the best of terms . . . had a little spat. I decided to ride back to the mine alone and not wait for him."

At least he didn't lie about their relationship. "Did you have your horse at Erik's?"

"Vat are you implying?" Kauffmann asked.

"That you went from the bar to Erik's, and shot poor Liam down like a dog."

"I rode back to the mine. Here I am, aren't I?"

That made Peckham smile. The man had his share of audacity.

"You could have ridden back up here after you shot Liam."

"My horse was tied outside the Kaiser. I rode straight up here. Ask the frog, Beauchamp."

Beauchamp was the bartender at the Kaiser. And Peckham had already asked him. "Beauchamp saw you leave, after you'd had a fight with Liam —"

"No fight, discussion. You ever haf a partner, Marshal?"

"Beauchamp saw you leave, but didn't know if your horse was outside or not."

"Keep asking. Someone saw it there. Der was people on the street. I had no reason to go to the Dutchman's. And no reason to shoot my partner. We argued once't in a while, but Liam and I was good friends."

"Didn't sound like it to Beauchamp."

"Friends have discussions. Some of them a little loud sometime. Partners too."

"Liam had a deed drawn, Gunter, and took five hundred dollars out of the bank. . . ."

"I would not sell for any five hundred dollars, Marshal . . . but it's enough to give some lout reason to rob . . . and kill . . . poor Liam."

"You got a shotgun?"

"Don't everyone in these mountains?"

146

"Probably, but I'd like to see yours."

"I get," he said, and spun on his heels and went inside. Peckham could hear some shuffling inside. He rested his hand on his gun butt as he waited for Kauffmann to return. He had no interest in ending up like Liam.

But Kauffmann returned with the shotgun in hand, broken with the barrels hanging down and the chambers exposed.

He handed it over to the marshal, who put the chambers up to his nose and took a whiff.

Nothing but gun oil. "Don't smell like it's been shot lately."

"Can't remember the last time."

"Somebody overheard you talking at Miss Betsylou's, to another man, something about shooting ol' Liam down on the trail."

"The hell you say," Gunter snapped. "I don't talk with nobody about shootin' nobody."

Peckham stood staring at him for a long moment, then turned and headed for his horse. When he'd mounted, he called out to Kauffmann, "You come see me next week when you come to town. I got more questions for you."

Kauffmann merely shrugged.

147

When he returned to his cabin, he noticed that the bleeding had started again from the hole in his side. But not so bad that the marshal could see it. Thank God he'd been smart enough to clean the scattergun, and had time to throw the bloody-holed shirt into the potbellied stove when he'd come back in to get the shotgun for Peckham.

None of them are smart enough to get old Gunter Kauffmann. None of them.

Twelve

It seemed like an eternity waiting for the band of Bloods to come. If they rode past, he and Silas had agreed, there would be no shooting. If they turned and followed the track up the creek, they'd wait until they got to the base off the waterfall, where the game trail led up to the meadow; then they'd give them what for.

Silas had made the women stay in the little cave with the horses, and had all three of the McGraws' rifles with him. He'd left the women with a pair of small pistols. Even at that, the rifles were all single-shots, and he'd have only three shots before he had to reload. Then again, the Sharps was good for five hundred yards, and he could get a couple of shots off before the average rifle was close enough to do him damage.

Sam had his Winchester 73, as well as his side arm. Enough cartridges to take the dozen down, if he scored with damn near every shot, which he knew by long experience was damned unlikely. He'd only been shot at a few times, but knew that when the lead was flying, sometimes your own aim was a little haphazard, particularly when the shooters were a bunch of wild painted Indians, screamin' and yellin' and comin' for your scalp. He vowed he'd make every shot count. He could, with the lever action and the revolver, throw a lot of lead if the fighting was in close, and Silas could pick them off at a long distance.

And they were well forted up. All in all, Sam felt pretty sure of himself. Then he glanced at the ridges surrounding the little meadow on three sides, over a hundred feet above. If the Indians got up there, there would be hell to pay.

They hunkered low as the hoofbeats neared, peering out between cracks in the rock forks they'd built.

The Bloods were led by a big man. Sam figured, by the way he sat in the well-decorated, elk-hide-covered saddle, that he could be a half head taller than himself. He was followed by the better part of a dozen fine-looking men. They were well painted, and even in the chill, half wore only breechclouts. All seemed to be carrying long arms, as well as tomahawks and a few spears.

Sam was about to let out a deep breath as it looked as if they would pass on by, but then a brave near the end of the procession reined his horse around and stared at the track leaving the creek and making its way into the willows. He yelled out, and it took a moment for the message to make its way to the front of the column, but in moments, they'd all returned and bunched up. Then they stared up at the opening in the cliff face and the wide rift where the meadow lay.

Sam glanced over at Silas, and saw him begin to raise his rifle above the rock wall. It looked like it was going to be a Katy-bar-the-door brawl.

Letting his breath out, Sam slipped his barrel through a large notch he'd left in his rock wall, and picked one of the men in front of the column to follow with his sights as they rode away from Deep Creek and began to work their way through the willows. They were within a hundred feet of Sam and Silas, and only fifty feet or so below, when the man in the lead pulled rein and pointed at Silas's position. The lead man, who Sam presumed was Hunting Hawk, dove from the saddle, just as the boom of the big Sharps shattered the stillness. Then he charged the cliff below on foot, going out of sight in a few leaps.

Sam fired at his man, who grabbed his side, dropped his rifle, and spurred his pony. As Sam levered in another shell, the band broke and went in every direction, crashing through the willows and few cottonwoods. He fired again at a fleeing man, and that one doubled over in the saddle, but also stayed mounted.

As he levered in for the third shot, Sam glanced over to see that Talking Woman had come to Silas's side, and was reloading the breechloading needle guns as he zeroed in on another man with his buffalo gun. Sam got off a third shot at a man zigging and zagging through the willows, but didn't know if he hit him or not.

Then all Sam could hear was retreating hoofbeats and see distant backs hunkered low in the saddles, and the rumps of horses. The Indians had retreated both up and down the creek.

Except for Hunting Hawk, who was somewhere below them. It seemed the old chief's medicine was still plenty strong.

"How'd you do?" Silas yelled at him.

"Got a piece of two of them at least. Don't know about the third. You?"

"Likewise. Damned old fool Hunting Hawk is down below somewheres. Let's chuck some rocks down and see if'n we can flush the ol' coon."

Then both of them dove for cover as a shot ricocheted off the rock wall behind them.

"This here is gonna slow down a mite, woman," Silas said to Talking Woman. "You skedaddle back to the cave now."

"You shoot, I load."

"Do as I say, woman."

"It is my nose," Talking Woman said, then repeated, "You shoot, I load."

Sam shook his head in sympathy, knowing that the Blackfeet — and he presumed the cousin tribes — cut a woman's nose off for being an adulteress. Silas didn't argue with this reasoning, and she stayed.

Silas eased up with the big buffalo gun, scanning the canyon walls across the creek. On both flanks, the Indians were moving up the walls two hundred yards up and down the creek.

"They's tryin' to get the angle on us," Silas called over to Sam. "Let's keep 'em low."

The Indians scrambled from tree to tree or boulder to boulder. On Silas's third shot, an Indian threw up his arms and

153

rolled backward down the steep incline.

The man hit the ground, then began crawling on all fours to get out of the line of fire. Sam glanced over, surprised that Silas didn't fire again to finish him off.

Silas caught his glance. "I learnt some things when I was packin' for the army. Old sergeant told me ofttimes it was better to have a wounded enemy than a dead'n."

"Why's that?"

"Well, they got to care for a wounded man. Dead one's no trouble."

"Makes sense," Sam said, again scanning the cliff sides across the creek. He saw a man leap from one tree to the next, making his way higher. He studied the location and saw a spot where he'd have to move twenty feet up a steep slope to the cover of the next tree, estimated the distance at two hundred twenty yards, and adjusted his sights. Then he patiently waited. Finally, the man broke from cover. Sam led him, and squeezed off a shot. His man went down and rolled back to where he'd started.

"Good shootin'," Silas called out; then several shots slammed into the rock cairns they'd built, and both of them hunkered low.

Silas cackled. Then backhanded his

mouth. Sam could see he was working a chaw, and chewing quite a bit faster than usual. "I figure there's six of 'em with holes. They'll be a mite more careful from here on."

Sam was wishing they'd carefully turn tail and go home, but he was sure that wouldn't happen, even though he and Silas had drawn a lot of blood.

For the rest of the afternoon, it was eerily quiet. When the sun set, they could hear old Hunting Hawk scramble away from his hideout below. But it was too dark to see him.

Silas wandered over to Sam's spot, finding a flat rock to use to cross the creek. "We won't hear from those ol' coons until dawn. They figure they can't find a way to the Great Father if they's kilt in the dark."

"I wish I was as sure of that as you."

"I kept about a foot of that old elk loin in my bedroll. I imagine the ladies is cookin' it up."

"I'll come back there to eat, but then I'm gonna park it out here so I can keep an ear tuned."

"Whatever makes y'all purr, ol' coon," Silas said, and strode out toward the cave.

Miss Helen and Miss Betsylou Maddigan sat on the porch watching the twilight fade. The sky over Phillipsburg had cleared, and the stars were beginning to blink.

There was little business, and none for Helen, so they'd retired to the porch with a cup of tea.

They sat in silence for a long while, enjoying the crisp cold, each with a shawl around her shoulders, until finally Helen spoke up. "Do you suppose Liam is up there somewhere?"

"I don't think Liam had a mean bone in his tall lanky body. So, if there's anyone who's gone to his reward in heaven, then Liam has."

"Then I guess I'll never see him again."

"Why do you say that, Helen? 'Cause you work in a place like this?"

Again, they were silent for a long time. Then Betsylou added, "You read the Good Book?"

"Not since I was a wee thing."

"Well, do you remember Mary Magdalen?"

"A little."

"Well, she was a woman who had to work for a living, just like you and me. She bathed Jesus' feet, and so far as is believed, she may still be at his feet in heaven."

"Well, I don't know about sitting at his feet for eternity, but I do hope I'll be able to hold hands with Liam and walk though some green meadows, when it's my time."

"You been doin' some mean talking about Gunter Kauffmann."

"You think I might not get to join Liam should I do harm to Gunter?"

"I didn't say that, Helen." Betsylou took a long sip of tea, then added, "But I imagine it wouldn't bode well for you, should you do harm to Mr. Kauffmann."

Helen was quiet for another long time. Then she finished her cup of tea, set the cup down, and rose to go back inside. At the door, she stopped and turned back to face Betsylou. "You know, it might just be worth it."

The door slammed behind her. Betsylou sat and watched the night, and began to hum "Rock of Ages." It was a melody not often heard at Miss Betsylou Maddigan's.

A half dozen men, obviously coming from one of the saloons in town, stumbled up to the picket fence and almost fell through the gate as they laughed and caroused.

Betsylou sighed deeply, then stood and stretched her arms and yawned. When she'd finished, she called out to the men,

"Hey, boys, come on in and taste the sweetness of life . . . and a little of my good whiskey."

After they'd eaten the roast loin, done to a turn on a stick in front of the fire, Sam wandered back out to his spot and spread out his buffalo robe. He was beginning to doze when he snapped to, hearing the cracking of a twig, and grabbed up his rifle.

"Only me," a soft voice said.

"Mary?"

"Yes, Mary. Sorry to startle you."

"No, no, I'm glad you came out." He moved over to a nearby rock. "Sit on the robe and rest a spell."

"You too."

"Pardon?"

"You sit on the robe with me. There is room for two." He readjusted the robe and she sat beside him, both leaning on a boulder.

They sat for a while just watching the night. Had it been under different circumstances, it would have been one of the happiest times Sam had known in a long, long time.

Finally, she spoke. "Sam . . . May I call you Sam?"

"Of course. Your English is excellent . . .

probably better than mine."

"I have spoken the white man's language since I was born."

"Of course, I didn't mean offense."

"None taken."

Again they were silent for a while. Then it was Sam who spoke. "I wanted to give you the hide . . . the elk hide. And I was going to give the horn to Talking Woman."

"I would gladly accept. Thank you. We will find it again."

"I wish I was as sure as you."

"If not, there will be many more." She smiled. "You should be careful what you give to a Blackfeet woman, Sam. Gifts can sometimes mean more than you white men know."

"I think I would enjoy giving you many gifts."

She changed the subject. "The sky has cleared. Many stars tonight. The moon will be out soon."

"And the Bloods won't come?"

"Not until dawn, if they come at all. You and my father have given them much reason to go home and lick wounds."

Sam was quiet for a moment. "I don't much favor killing people . . . any people."

"Even the plains people?"

"Any people."

"Then, with luck, you only gave them reason to spend a long while under their teepee, having their women tend their wounds."

"I don't know. The one I hit up on the mountainside went down hard. I've shot a lot of critters, and I'd guess that was a killing shot."

"And I also don't like seeing things killed, but it is the Great Father's way. The animals are there for the people, and must be killed to fill the pot. When men come upon you, meaning to do harm, sometimes killing is the only thing they understand."

"And these Bloods?"

"They follow their great chief, who follows only his man pride. He thinks he is without weakness, or so he tells his people and any other who will listen. His weakness is his pride. Still, you did not see him leave his spot below until it was too dark to shoot. Or so my father told me. That is not the action of a man who truly believes he cannot be touched by harm."

"I've seen some tough men, Mary, but none tougher than a forty-four caliber."

"Then maybe it's time we showed Hunting Hawk the same."

He thought on this for a while, and began to form a plan. Finally, he responded.

"Maybe. Still, I hope they're long gone in the morning."

"As do I. Mother will be worried." She rose, and Sam felt there was a vacuum beside him. Before she started back, she smiled at him, a smile he could little more than sense in the darkness, but it was in her words. "Thank you, Sam, for the hide, even if we had to leave it behind."

"As you said, there will be another."

"Sleep well," she said, and moved away into the darkness.

"I doubt it," he said, but doubted if she heard.

Morning came with the sunlight creeping down the west side of the cleft, with no sign of the Bloods. They ate all but the very last handful of their jerky and a few dry biscuits, knowing that any time the meadow would be kicking up dust from a barrage of Blood gunfire.

But nothing.

Sam and Silas were both in position behind their rock piles, waiting.

Finally, in midmorning, Silas called over to Sam, "I think they figure on starvin' us out of here."

"You don't think they've gone?"

" 'Bout the same chance that grulla of

your'n will grow a horn and be one o' them unicorns."

"We bloodied 'em up pretty good yesterday," Sam said, hopefully.

"Which only made old Hunting Hawk get his hackles up."

"So, how long do we wait?"

"Another full day after this'n; then I say we try and sneak out in the dead of night."

Sam was quiet for a while, then called over, "I never was much good at waitin'."

"You wanna chaw?"

"No, thanks."

Sam lay on his back, watching the cliffs above, from where he knew the most devastating attack might come.

Here and there sprigs of brush grew out of cracks in the cliffs. The little winter birds had come, he noticed. He'd always enjoyed watching nature change seasons, particularly early spring and the coming of winter. These little guys had dark brown heads and lighter brown bodies. He called them winter sparrows, and wondered what their proper names were.

High above, a bald eagle circled, with a pair of crows harassing him mercilessly. With noble aplomb, he ignored them.

As Sam studied the cliff side, he noticed a couple of places where cracks extended all the way down the cliff to the meadow. He wondered if he could climb one of those cracks. If so, he could drop a line down for the others. But he couldn't see high enough to know what he would face once he got a hundred feet up. The tops of the cliffs curved away.

Finally, when the sun was at its apex, directly to the south of the little canyon, Sam stood and stretched. He'd been cramped in the hidey-hole for hours, and his muscles were beginning to ache.

"Careful, ol' coon," Silas cautioned. "Them ol' boys —"

The slap of a bullet spun Sam, and he went down, as the echo of the shot reverberated across the little meadow.

Thirteen

"You hit?" Silas yelled, and jumped up and ran to Sam.

Another shot rang out, kicking dust up beside them, and both of them crawled to Sam's hole.

Sam felt his side, realizing that the shot had creased him, cutting a notch in his leather belt. His hand came away covered with blood. "Just touched, but it burns like hell."

"You need it tended?"

"No, I think it'll stop and scab over."

"Good thing it didn't pop yer melon. Y'all stay low, now. You're a fair hand an' I don't favor losing you. Miss Mary's takin' a shine. And even Talking Woman is learnin' to tolerate yer ugly hide."

"Yes, sir. I'm staying lower than a snake's belly."

"Like I said, they's still out there. Ol' Hunting Hawk won't be headin' back to

164

his women until my hide is tacked on the teepee." Silas guffawed, then added, "Give them something to worry about whilst I get back."

Sam stuck his barrel through the hole he'd left in the rock pile and searched the mountainside and cliffs across the stream, but could see nothing. He fired off a shot nonetheless, and Silas scrambled back.

"They are pretty well hid out," he yelled to Silas. "Did you see where that shot came from? I'd like to repay the favor."

"Nope. They's had time to hole up. But I'd guess a couple of them ol' dogs is a-climbing the mountain on this side to try an' get above us. They'll be hell to pay when they do."

"If they can."

"They can. Question is, can they get where they can get a shot? Them ol' rounded shoulders on these cliffs is mighty slick. You want a chaw?"

"Don't chaw, Silas. Never have, never gonna start."

"Good. More fer me."

Sam made himself comfortable on his back on the buff hide again. As he felt his side, making sure it was no worse than he'd said, he realized the bullet had holed his shirt in two places.

It had been too damn close for comfort.

It stayed quiet until nightfall; then all hell broke loose.

As they gave up their posts and were headed back to the cave, rocks, then boulders, began to rain into the meadow. Staying close to the walls, they scurried to the cave.

"Damn the flies," Silas said as they got to safety. "They probably can't get close enough to the edge to shoot at us, so they's raining the mountain down on our heads."

"Maybe they'll soon run outta boulders to shove over."

"Hope so, that could make a fella a mite nervous."

"Can I turn the horses out?" Mary asked her father.

"Best wait until we've had a long spell without no boulders."

"We have made some soup from the last of the jerky. Then we go hungry. We can dig some root from that small patch of cattails near the pond. That will last us another day."

"Somethin' will turn up . . . always does," Silas said, but didn't sound convinced.

After downing his soup, Sam made his

way back out to his indentation. All day he'd been thinking about what he could do to make this end, and he thought he had it figured out.

He waited until the moon had risen and disappeared again in the west. When he figured it must be somewhere between three and four in the morning, he removed his boots and made his way past Silas's hideout to where the trail topped out from the creek meadow below.

As quietly as he could, he carefully worked his way down to the flat keeping one hand on the steep bank next to him. He stopped every four steps and listened, just as if he were hunting. But nothing. No sound disturbed the silence, not even crickets. It was too cold, well below freezing. After taking fifteen minutes to drop the fifty feet to the creek bottom, he again spent more than a minute just standing and straining to hear, then headed into the willows lining Deep Creek. He presumed the Indians had not bothered with a guard at the foot of the trail as they had men stationed both upstream and down. And they presumed if he and the McGraws made a run for it, it would be giving the whip to the horses.

They didn't anticipate one man on foot,

heading into the jaws of the Indian encampment.

When Hunting Hawk sneaked away the night before, he had made his way back to the east. Sam figured the Indian camp, if they had a camp, would be that way. Probably around the bend a couple of hundred yards upstream.

Now, to get there without being discovered.

The moon had been up and down, and it was as dark as a proverbial foot up a bull's butt.

But it was hard going through the willows without making a lot of sound. The muddy spots wanted to suck at his stocking feet, and the snow patches crunched underfoot. The creek, tumbling over the occasional boulder, helped cover any noise he made. As did the roar of the waterfall behind him.

As soon as he'd traveled a hundred yards, and could see a ways around the next bend, he heard a horse whinny, then fifty more yards, and he heard the soft nicker of a number of horses chortling at each other. He made his way out of the willows and up an escarpment on the same side of the creek as their makeshift fort.

When he was twenty feet or so up the

slope, he could see a glow, he presumed embers of the evening fire. He figured the distance, as well as he could in the darkness, at somewhere around one hundred yards.

He dared not get closer, as he was positive they'd have a guard posted.

So he waited. Dawn was late coming as winter was growing near, and his feet were freezing. He folded them under him and sat on them the best he could, then snuggled down between two small boulders. He dozed a little, but the thought of Silas being staked out snapped him fully awake every time his eyes began to close.

Finally, the first thin rays of light began to outline the mountaintops to the east. Someone stirred the fire, and added wood to it, and as soon as it caught flame, he was able to make out the shapes of a couple of men moving about. He rejudged the distance at no more than seventy-five yards. Closer than he meant to get. It was less than fifteen minutes when the red of morning over the mountains to the east seemed to call for blood. A man approached the fire who seemed larger than the rest. Sam was sure it was Hunting Hawk, but he could make out no features yet. Not wanting his quest to be in vain, he decided to wait another ten minutes. Shooting the wrong Indian would not serve his purpose. The blood call of the eastern dawn began to fade from red to pink, when he decided there was no doubt. The man walked to the side of the camp deeper into darkness — Sam feared that he was walking away to somewhere he couldn't be seen — but the big Indian relieved himself in the brush then walked back, and turned his back to the fire and folded his hands behind him.

There were only four men on their feet in the camp when Sam laid the Winchester across a boulder. He zeroed in on the man's chest for a moment, then remembered what Silas had said about a wounded man being a burden to the enemy. . . . Besides, even a crippling wound should convince Hunting Hawk of his vulnerability. And his vulnerability should convince the rest that following him might be nothing more than a short trip to the happy hunting grounds.

He dropped the sights to his right thigh, and squeezed off a shot. Hunting Hawk spun backward, falling across the fire and kicking up a shower of sparks, but rolling quickly out. The shot reverberated up and down the canyon, and the Indians went into a frenzy, diving for their firearms, then firing blindly into every crack and cranny above them.

Hawk cried out like a ruptured duck, and a deep feeling of satisfaction flooded Sam. Then reality set back in and he figured it would be unwise to wait to see anymore. He headed down the escarpment of rock, stumbling and falling hard one time, but he was as quickly back on his feet. He ran as if hell were on his heels, and he was sure it was. Before he disappeared behind the willows, shots kicked up mud on the trail behind him. They did not discourage his retreat.

A thin game trail worked its way along the high side of the river willows, and he followed it as closely as he could, but he could barely make it out in the dim light of dawn. He was almost to the trail leading up to the meadow when he heard pounding footfalls behind him. He'd always heard that some Indians could run like the wind, and this one was proving it; he was about to catch up with him.

Sam spun, dropped to one knee, and fired three rapid shots behind him, without really having a target in the shaded darkness, but knowing the track he'd taken. He heard a wounded cry, but again didn't wait for any confirmation of his hit.

Then he made his way, scrambling on all threes, with one hand holding the rifle. Up, up, until he reached the switchback. Shards of rock splattered him as a shot ricocheted off the wall behind him. He didn't hesitate again until at the top of the rise he crashed over the makeshift fence Silas had put up to keep the horses in the meadow.

"What the hell!" he heard Silas call out.

"It's me, old man! Don't be shootin' me! Watch the trail."

"Where the hell you been, ol' coon?"

"Keep your head down. I stirred up the rattlesnake's den."

Before he'd finished the sentence, four more shots slammed into the walls around their encampment, and both of them dove for their little forts.

"You did do a right good job gettin' 'em buzzin'," Silas said. "I thought maybe you done lit a shuck . . . 'ceptin you wouldn't a left that ugly blue horse behind."

"I got to thinkin' about something you and Miss Mary had to say yesterday."

"What's that?"

"Well, I put a bullet in ol' Hunting Hawk's hide. Maybe the rest of 'em will quit now."

"You kilt him?"

"Nope, but I probably gave him a limp he'll keep the rest of his days."

"Why the hell didn't you kill the old fool?"

"Now, Silas, remember what you said about a wounded man being a burden?"

"Yep . . . but that don't apply to Hunting Hawk."

"Shoulda said something yesterday," Sam said, then smiled to himself.

Silas was quiet for a long spell, then finally cleared his throat and spoke. "You want a chaw?"

This time, Sam didn't bother to answer. He was busy trying to catch any movement in the creek bed below.

A few more boulders crashed into their meadow that day, but no more shots rang out. They made do on roasted cattail roots and soup made of peeled cattail stalks. Sam was pleasantly surprised to find it tasty, as they still had some salt left.

That afternoon, as they waited for the sun to set, Sam, getting bored, made some conversation. "How long do you figure we can hold out?"

"Hell, for a month of Sundays, I suppose, if'n we don't get ourselves shot full of holes or have our head bones cracked open by some boulder."

"How so? We'll be out of cattails real soon."

"Hell, ol' coon, that grulla of yours would last us most of a month. He looks real tasty."

"The hell you say. I'd carve up your liver before I'd eat on Blue."

Old Silas laughed and slapped his thighs. Then he managed, "Well, ol' coon, one of them paint ponies then."

"Humph," Sam managed, but knew the old man was right. With water, and almost no feed left for the animals, it would be horse meat if they continued to be trapped here.

He hoped against hope his plan had worked, and that the Bloods would ride out soon, with their discredited chief in tow.

Sam felt lucky he'd managed to get this far with only a scratch on his side. The small wound was healing well, and unless it went green, he expected little trouble from it.

As hard as he'd searched, and he'd talked to everyone in town including the town drunks, Marshal Clark Peckham had been unable to turn up any leads. Although many had heard the shot, no one had seen anything, including anyone escaping. No one remembered what time Gunter Kauffmann had ridden out of town.

Since sporting women worked halfway through the night, he decided to find out how alert they were in the early morning. As soon as he'd had his coffee, which he took at Frenchy's Fine Dining Emporium, he walked out to Miss Betsylou's. He'd never been inside Betsylou's, never closer than the front gate. But business was business.

No one was stirring at seven in the morning, but the front door was unlocked. He barged in and took the stairs two at a time. He opened the first door he came to, and a robust girl with stringy blond hair and a face as round as a dinner plate, looked up from her nest of feather comforter and pillows.

"It's a bit early . . ." she mumbled.

"Miss Helen's room?"

She looked a little affronted, but waved him away. "Last door on the left."

He closed the door and moved down the hall, then threw the indicated door open and walked in and perched himself on the end of the brass wire bed.

She looked up, rubbed her eyes, then tucked the pillow under her head so she could focus on him.

"Good morning, Miss Helen . . . or should I say Miss Maureen?"

"I'll answer to either."

"Now, tell me again, when did you make your agreement with Gunter? The same night both Gunter and Liam were here?"

Helen sat up and fluffed up a pillow, then put it behind her back, and settled her eyes on Peckham again. "Marshal, I would make no deal with Gunter Kauffmann if he were the kaiser himself. If you're not here on Miss Betsylou's business, then I'm getting up and going downstairs and making coffee. Would you care for a cup?"

As she spoke she flipped back the covers and climbed out of bed. She wore a flimsy lace thing that one could clearly see through, particularly when she walked in front of the window with its morning sun streaming in.

Marshal Clark Peckham began to redden. "No . . . I . . ."

But he didn't turn away. He couldn't bring himself to, as he'd never seen a woman quite so nicely shaped. He'd never seen a woman so nearly in her natural state except for his wife, Sarah.

As he stood uncomfortably with his eyes

176

fixed on the shapely woman, Clark Peckham realized that his wife was a little more amply endowed than Miss Helen. Of course, she was ample over her whole body, not just in the right places.

Miss Helen picked up a tortoiseshell comb and began running it through her long dark red locks, her breasts bobbing nicely as she did so. "I've never seen you at a loss for words, Clark. Now, do you want a cup of coffee?"

She started for the door.

"You going down like that?" he mumbled.

"There's no one here this time of morning, 'cept for you. Doesn't bother you, does it, Marshal?"

"I'll go on down and wait for you to get dressed."

She laughed, and he again blushed. Then she added, "I'll just put on a wrap."

He almost ran for the door as she began pulling the lace nightgown over her head.

When she came into the kitchen he was seated at a ladderback kitchen chair, his hat in his lap. She couldn't help wondering if the hat was in that particular place in order to conceal his interest.

She pumped up a potful of water and threw in a handful of coffee, stoked up the fire in the cast-iron stove, added a couple of sticks from the wood bin, placed the pot on the stove, then walked over and sat across the table from him.

"It'll take a minute. Now, what were you asking?"

"Gunter?" Peckham was still a little taken aback, but managed to get it out. "Gunter Kauffmann, you and he made a deal? . . ."

"No, Marshal. No deal." Then she smiled coyly at him. "That's not really what you came here for this morning, now, is it, Clark?"

Fourteen

Miss Helen winked at Marshal Clark Peckham.

He stammered, "Yes, finding out who killed Liam Stranahan certainly is why I came here."

She let him stew in his own juice for a moment, then rose and went to a cupboard and fetched two white pottery cups.

When the stammer left him, he continued, "I'll tell you the truth, Miss Helen, I can't find a thing that helps me find this killer. Your old friend, your good customer, Gunter, is going to get away with this, and you're going to have him as a partner. A murderer as a partner, if you don't fess up."

"No deal, Marshal. I've never fired a gun in my life, and don't own one. And Gunter's no longer any customer of mine. You need to put the shackles on Gunter Kauffmann and drag him down to your jail —"

"Miss Helen, I'd like that but I don't have any evidence. Nobody saw him near that barn. I rode up there yesterday. He has a shotgun, but it didn't smell as if it'd been shot in a month of Sundays."

The pot began to bubble, and she rose to stand beside the stove.

He glanced out the window to keep from staring. "Have you gone to see Willingham at the express yet?"

"No. I told you, I have no interest in what Liam might have left me. I loved Liam because he was Liam, not for what he owned, and surely not because of any will."

"Go see Parker Willingham, and take care of business." He rose and walked to the door. "Liam wanted you to have it." Then he paused and turned back. "You know his brother, Samuel?"

"Liam never mentioned a brother."

"Well, he left one-quarter to you, and one-quarter to his brother, Samuel."

"So each of us has a twenty-five percent interest?"

"That's right. If you hear from this Samuel, you come runnin', you hear?"

"That's fine. You think he might have had something to do with Liam's killing?"

"I have no idea, but I'd like to find him

and have a little talk."

"If I hear from him . . ."

"Might be wise of you. I've got a wanted handbill from Bozeman on Sam Stranahan. Murder and robbery, five-hundred-dollar reward. He's killed before, and he could have killed Liam. If I was you, I'd watch my back. If it wasn't Gunter and it wasn't you who shot Liam, it was surely this Sam. And both of them would gain if you was toes up. There are plenty who don't fancy havin' to do business with womenfolk."

He walked out, and she stared after him. She hadn't considered the fact that if Gunter had killed for a half interest in the mine, he might just as well kill for a quarter.

And Sam, who the devil was Sam?

Other than a wanted killer.

Rusty Pacovsky and the Cree trackers saddled early and rode hard, changing horses three times by the time they reached Deep Creek and the old Indian trading trail.

They studied the trail for a mile up its length, looking for sign of recent traffic, but found none.

"Looks like we beat 'em here," Rusty said, a satisfied look on his face.

"If they come this way," Little Ears said.

They rode up the trail until it began to climb up into the high mountains, then found a spot on a rise, but with their backs enjoying the protection of a higher cliff. It was a fine spot with plenty of firewood and a good view of the trail below for almost a mile.

The weather was clear, but had gone cold. A fire would be welcome as all of them were sweated through. They rubbed down and staked the horses, and made a little camp against the cliff side.

Pacovsky pulled his saddle and bedroll and threw it up against the rock wall. Charley Mad-in-the-Morning went to pick up firewood, but Little Ears stayed close by.

He noticed the bottleneck sticking out of Rusty's bedroll, and his eyes flared with interest.

"Whiskey?" Little Ears asked, then licked his lips.

Rusty reached over with a foot and toed the bottle deeper into the bedroll.

"That's fer snakebite, Little Ears. You keep yer damned hands off'n it. We got work."

"You got whiskey," the Indian said, and glared at Rusty.

"Yeah, and I'm keeping it bottled up till

we finish our business."

"You got whiskey," Little Ears said again, then walked over and gathered up the lead rope of his and Charley's horses, and led them away to find a place with better graze. "Got whiskey," Little Ears mumbled again as he moved away.

Rusty eyed the bedroll. "Damn fool." He chastised himself. For a moment, he thought about jerking the quart out, taking a couple of long draws, and pouring the rest of it into the sand, but then thought better. "Hell, I'll just keep them out of it."

But he knew that would be easier said than done.

After the sun sank, and before the moon rose, Sam heard one unshod horse clatter the rocks as he trotted by below, going downstream. In less than an hour, he heard what he guessed was three sets of hoof-beats going back upstream.

He rose from his hideout and crossed the meadow back to the cave, where Silas sat by a fire with the ladies. "Something is going on out there. I heard a horse pass an hour ago, going downstream, then just now three came back upstream."

"Sounds like they may be gatherin' up. Let's hope it's to ride out, but if not, could be they decided the only way to get at our hides is to come at night."

"I better get back to my hole," Sam said, and headed out.

"Be careful, Sam," Miss Mary called after him.

Silas rose and stretched. "Best I go too, but let's hope ol' Huntin' Hawk has had his fill."

"Pray so," Talking Woman said.

But there was no more sound, other than the occasional screech of a nighthawk, for the next three hours. Silas finally rose and made his way across the small creek to Sam's spot. "I think it's time we ride out of here."

"Sounds right to me. I think they've left, or at least they're all gathered up in their camp upstream."

"You keep an ear out here and I'll get the ladies to packin' up."

"Let's be out of here before moonrise."
Silas nodded.

When he led the horses out, Sam realized that old wiley Silas had tied cloth around, or bagged, each of their hooves. They made little noise on the rocks.

Silas had noted that Mary's horse was still gimpy. He mounted up, then offered his daughter a lift up, but Sam stopped him with a loud whisper.

"This stud's the strongest. Mary can ride behind me."

"Suits me," Silas said, and Mary hurried over and with Sam's arm-up, swung onto the horse's rump behind him.

"You lead out, Silas," Sam whispered, but Silas was already on the little trail heading down.

Sam let Talking Woman fall in behind her husband, and he and Mary took up the rear. Mary's horse followed.

Quietly, at a slow walk, they worked their way back down to Deep Creek, then moved off downstream. After they'd gone a quarter mile, Silas dismounted and pulled the cloth mufflers from the horses' hooves.

He swung back into the saddle, then said in a loud whisper, "Let's keep up a canter for a while, until we got some distance between us and the Bloods."

As they took up the pace, Sam could not help getting a twinge when Mary was forced to wrap her arms tightly around him, shove her thighs with her buckskin skirt riding high up against his legs, and press her bosom to his back. He was almost sorry when Silas again reined back to a walk, and Mary relaxed her grip and backed away.

Silas reined back and let Sam catch up. "They's another little side crick up near the mouth of the canyon. I say we head up it a ways and make a cold camp till morning. Then if we ain't heard naught of the Bloods, we'll fire up and have the last of the coffee."

"Sounds right to me."

And they made it safely there.

Norval Hutchins, Gordon Pendergast, and Tucker Stark had known each other since they were pups down in Bannock days, when Sheriff Henry Plummer and his band had been strung up by an angry vigilante committee. The three wet-behind-the-ears young bandits were not among the more than twenty, including the sheriff, who'd had their necks stretched. The three of them had fled town in different directions, one to Canada, one to Wyoming, and one to Oregon, but they'd all found their way back to Montana over the years. They were no longer novices, but now considered themselves hard-boiled. All had killed, and escaped; Tucker Stark had many notches on his rifle and revolver. And all had heard rumors that Phillipsburg had risen from the grave and discoveries were again being made. That would mean there were many mud-grubbing miners there ripe for the picking. And Pendergast had relatives who lived down Flint Creek a few miles from Phillipsburg and were raising hogs.

Hutchins and Pendergast had met up again in Bozeman, and had been up to some petty mischief when they were hired by the deputy sheriff, Rusty Pacovsky, to partici- pate in a stage holdup. They'd worked for the law before, doing much the same kind of jobs, and were no stranger at it. But they were unhappy when Pacovsky shot down his own brother, who was riding shotgun messenger on the Overland. The job had gone from robbery to murder, and they weren't being paid well enough for killing.

Still, they'd been more than pleased to take their money from the sheriff, and take his advice to get the hell out of town.

When they arrived in Phillipsburg, and were on their way to O'Mally's Saloon, they got a good laugh, seeing a handbill on the front of the marshal's office. A wanted handbill for some fella named Sam Stranahan. A fellow wanted for the crime they and Deputy Rusty Pacovsky had com- mitted.

"Hell's fire, Hutchins," Pendergast said with a guffaw, "wouldn't it be a hoot if you and I made five hundred for shooting down the old boy who's wanted for a bit of our own handiwork?"

"That would be somethin' all right. But I'll bet if'n that old boy has anything upstairs, he's halfway to Oregon by now."

When they entered O'Mally's, they bellied up to the bar and were surprised to come face-to-face with an old comrade-in-arms. This was the first time since Bannock that they'd run into Stark, and the three of them were having a good old time, recounting stories of past glories, while downing a bottle of cheap rye.

After finishing the first bottle, and when well into the second, Stark suggested they give the wanton ladies at Miss Betsylou's a visit. It was a unanimous vote.

They stumbled out of O'Mally's, on the far side of Phillipsburg from Betsylou's, and mounted up for the short ride up Broadway to Brewery, where Miss Betsylou's crowned a small hill in all its Victorian splendor.

At Betsylou's it was business as usual, with the exception that Betsylou and Miss Helen were enjoying a cup of tea in the kitchen. The public rooms, the drawing and dining rooms of the fine house were almost at capacity even with all the girls other than Helen upstairs and occupied. Since Miss Helen was surely by far the most popular of the girls, she and Betsylou had agreed to raise her price from one token to two. She wasn't as busy as she had been before, but she was making more money nonetheless.

One-Eyed George Choi was the only Chinaman allowed into Betsylou's. He was not there for the usual reason, but because he was an excellent poker player. And he'd made an arrangement with Betsylou: he would give his own stake and all she had to do was give him a seat at the table when a game was in the offing. Usually, she would take a seat for a few hands, then would give the seat up to One-Eyed George, telling the crowd that he was a good friend. Which he was, as George had loaned her a good portion of the money needed to buy the place. Her inviting him into the game quelled the objections of the others. George was not allowed in any of the other games in town, and didn't care, as the white devils who came to Betsylou's were usually drunk, and it was a simple job and great joy to relieve them of their hard-earned.

When he entered the establishment, One-Eyed George went straight to the kitchen as usual, and the customers presumed he was kitchen help. His elevated status in the community should have been obvious, as he wore a crimson silk shirt that hung below his ample buttocks, and his round face was punctuated by a red silk eye patch, embroidered with a green dragon's head. On a gold chain around his thick neck hung a finely carved Chinese-character jade pendant, which he had told Betsylou meant long life, but actually meant death to enemies. His black queue was thickly braided and hung to his waist, and although he sported the billowing trousers of a Chinaman, he wore black polished boots rather than the usual sandals. On his hip, mostly hidden by the long shirt, he wore a dagger with a gold handle.

He took his place at the kitchen table and Betsylou brought him a glass with a generous shot of whiskey, the only drink he would consume until the poker was over . . . if there was to be a game tonight.

Shortly after he arrived, three unshaven men entered and bellied up to the short bar. They each had a drink in hand by the time Betsylou returned to the public rooms. An excellent judge of character, she eyed them carefully and deemed them trouble. They appeared to be drifters or cattle hands, but each wore well-polished side arms, which hung a little low for a drifter or drover.

Not one to avoid whatever needed attending, Betsylou walked right over to the three. "You fellas just get into town?" Then she realized she'd seen one of them, the tallest and thinnest. He was not a man you'd quickly forget.

"Why, yes, ma'am, we surely did," the tall one said. He was sallow-faced, with a hawk nose and eyes as piercing as that predator.

A quick chill rattled her backbone. "Haven't I seen you around here before?" She stuck out a hand to shake. "I'm Betsylou Maddigan."

"Stark, Tucker Stark, and these are my associates, Hutchins and Pendergast."

"Nice to meet you fellows," she said, but it didn't ring true. "Haven't I seen you here before, Mr. Stark?"

"No. No, ma'am, my first visit. Just rode into town."

He lied; she knew he'd been here before, but only for a quick drink at the bar. She lied in return, "Well, we're happy to have you fellows. I'd appreciate it if you'd hang your firearms on the pegs outside on the front porch. We're a peaceable establishment."

One of the others answered. "Yes, ma'am, we'll get around to it."

"And you are?"

"Pendergast."

"That's fine, Mr. Pendergast." She flashed him an empty smile. "So long as you get around to it before you go upstairs with one of my girls, or before you have another drink."

They each nodded, but gave her a hard look.

She went to mingle with the other customers, then sidled up beside Helen, who was flashing a smile and batting her eyes at some potential customers. "You see that fella?" Betsylou nodded in Stark's direction.

"The one who looks like he should be an undertaker?"

"That's the one. He looks more like one who keeps the undertaker busy. I've been trying to remember when I saw him, and I think it was the night Liam stayed here with you."

"I don't remember seeing him."

"You was upstairs most of the night."

Betsylou moved on and chatted with the men, mostly to see if she could get a poker game started. In moments, she and three others had taken a seat at one of two round oak tables, and the gold and silver pieces and the cards were on the table.

It wasn't long, as all the one-token girls were occupied, before Pendergast and Stark wandered over and took a seat, each putting twenty dollars on the table and asking to be dealt in. Introductions were made and the men gave each other appraising nods.

The game was five-card stud, with Miss Betsylou keeping the deal, and dealer to ante a quarter on the first hand, and the ante but not the deal to rotate around the table. She won and lost a couple of hands, then turned her seat over to One-Eyed George, who had appeared out of the kitchen.

George picked up the cards to deal, and without hesitation, dealt like a riverboat gambler.

Stark had watched this all with astonishment, and finally got his tongue back. "Hold on," he challenged, standing at the same time. "I ain't playing with no Chinee." He laid a hand on the butt of the revolver still strapped on his hip, and slipped it partway from its holster, to add emphasis to what he'd said.

Fifteen

Betsylou Maddigan came to One-Eyed George's aid before he could respond to Tucker Stark's demand.

"Mr. Stark, George Choi has been playing cards here since the place opened, and he's welcome at my table. If you object, you're welcome to go down the hill to do your drinking and card playin'. You must think George too good a poker player?"

Stark glared at her, then back at the Chinaman. "By all that's holy . . . Hell, deal the cards, you heathen, and I'll have that googaw on your neck in my pocket before the night's over." He sat back down, but it was obvious he was perturbed.

"Remember," Betsylou added, before she turned back to the bar, "no more liquor until you take that belt outside."

Stark merely stared at her with those cold eyes; then he turned back to the game. "I'll play with you, Chinee boy, but

194

we're gonna be passing the deal."

George merely shrugged, and dealt.

Two of the other three men at the table were locals: Hardy McGregor was a driver for the Overland, and William Smithson was the local banker. McGregor was a single man and Smithson a widower, and mostly enjoyed Betsylou's for the card games and for the occasional romp in the feathers with the ladies. Ambrose Toynbee was a drummer, a traveling man, and new to the game. He was a diminutive man with a narrow brimmed bowler hat perched in his lap that normally covered a balding head. He sold needles, thread, and other ladies' personal items. His eyes lay a little close to his nose, he had a twitch that made him a lousy poker player, and both gave him the look of a nervous ferret.

After a couple of hands that amounted to little, Stark got the deal. On the first round of betting, with only the hole card and one faceup, both One-Eyed George and Stark had an ace showing. As the first ace bets, George threw in a five-dollar gold piece. Stark matched him, but eyed him suspiciously as the others dropped out.

On the next card, George received a four and Stark a deuce. George threw in another five-dollar gold piece.

"What the hell are you so proud of?" Stark mumbled, as George dealt the fourth cards. This time it was a queen for George, and another deuce for Stark.

Stark smiled broadly.

"Pair is betting," George said.

"I know 'pair is betting,'" Stark snapped. "You think I'm stupid as a Chinaman?"

"No," George said politely. "Celestials vely stupid. Bet, please."

This time it was Stark who threw out another five-dollar gold piece, leaving him only five dollars on the table. George had no way of knowing that it was Stark's last five dollars.

The fifth card was a jack for Stark and another ace for George.

George's expression never changed, but Stark was smiling broadly.

"Bet, please," George said, and Stark pushed out his last five-dollar gold piece.

"Vely good," George said. "I see, I raise twenty dolla."

The table quieted; then the whole room did so, as One-Eyed George pushed twenty-five dollars into the pot. Stark had no more money on the table, and he began to redden. Then he snapped, "Wait!" and shoved the table back and walked into the drawing room, where Pendergast and

196

Hutchins stood by the bar, talking to one of the girls who'd returned from upstairs.

Stark shoved his way through the other men in the room. "I need a gold eagle."

"Twenty dollars," Pendergast said. "What the hell for? You taking on all the girls in the house three or four times?"

"Poker game."

"What the hell kind of hand do you have that's worth twenty dollars?"

"Do you have twenty dollars?"

"Damn near my last twenty. Let me see your cards."

Stark shoved his way back to the dining room and took his seat. Pendergast studied the table for a moment, then knelt and looked at Stark's down card, another jack, making two pairs for Stark. Pendergast smiled, and dug in his pocket for his last eagle, then flipped it into the middle of the table.

"That's a call," Stark said, smiling. "I paid to see 'em."

"Aw, vely good," George said, and turned over his third ace.

Stark reddened, then rose slowly from the table.

"Ain't gonna lose my last to some damn fat Chinee fool."

With this, the drummer, Ambrose

Toynbee, rose, pocketed his money quickly, backed away from the table, and disappeared into the crowd.

Betsylou had watched the hands proceed, and quickly moved to Stark's side. "That's enough of that, Mr. Stark. You lost fair and square."

"No way," Stark said, easing his hand toward the revolver at his hip. Betsylou beat him there and covered the handle of the revolver with her own hand, interfering with his ability to draw the weapon.

"Please, Mr. Stark, just leave peaceably."

He glared at her, then lashed out and slapped her so hard she went to the floor in a heap, her eyes rolling up in her head. The room fell deadly silent as he slipped the big revolver from its holster and centered the muzzle on George's chest. "Now shove all your money across the table."

George quickly shoved the table money into the pot.

"All of it, Chinee boy."

George dug into his pockets and produced another stack of gold coins, almost two hundred dollars.

Stark's eyes sparked and he swung the muzzle from player to player. "The rest of you fellas might as well put whatever money you have in that pile." The banker did so willingly, but McGregor merely snarled at Stark.

"You too, Scotty," Stark snapped.

"Not likely," McGregor said, and rose to his feet. As tall as Stark was, the lanky Overland Stage driver was taller by two inches. And he, too, wore a big revolver.

Stark lost his smile, swung the muzzle to the big man's chest, and pulled the trigger. Everyone jumped back at least a full step, but McGregor was blown back against the dining room wall. Wide-eyed, unbelieving, he grasped a handful of curtains as he sank to the floor, pulling them and the rod above to the carpet with him, and leaving a streak of blood on the wall from the exit wound of the big slug.

One-Eyed George kicked his chair back and bolted for the kitchen door, then was blown on through it as Stark fired again, taking him in the middle of his back. The banker, Smithson, stood and held his hands out in front of him, to show Stark he had no weapon, or as if he could fend off the bullet, but couldn't do so as Stark fired a third time. He went to the floor gurgling with a hole in his throat, then crawled a couple of feet before collapsing.

Before he could fire again, Betsylou, who'd awakened from the blow, latched on to Stark's leg and sank her teeth into his calf like a crazed wolverine. He screamed and clubbed her viciously with the heavy revolver.

The rest of the men took the opportunity offered by Stark's lowered revolver, and a half dozen fell upon him. In moments, he was beaten to the floor.

His good friends, Pendergast and Hutchins, took advantage of the melee to sneak outside, mount their horses, and ride back down the hill to find another saloon. As far as they were concerned, they'd had nothing to do with it, and they had no interest in getting shot up or having their necks stretched for Tucker Stark. Hell, he'd never been that good a friend anyway.

When they reached the road and mounted up, Pendergast turned to Hutchins. "That's a fine gray ol' Stark rode, and he won't be needin' it, looks like. . . ."

"If you don't want him, I do," Hutchins said, so Pendergast dismounted and untied Stark's horse, and then led him away, whistling at their newfound fortune.

"Damned if I didn't get my twenty back," Pendergast said, with a chuckle.

In moments, Stark was trussed up with curtain ties and was being booted outside and down Broadway. While most of the miners and townspeople rode, he stumbled to the marshal's office and the awaiting cell. A few of them wanted to hang him right there, but cooler heads prevailed.

Helen had watched the whole thing from a perch at the bar in the drawing room, and it was only when the room cleared out that she saw that Miss Betsylou still on the floor, lying in a rapidly growing pool of blood from the gash on her head.

"Oh my God," Helen screamed, and yelled for the other girls. "One of you run for the doctor, and the rest of you help me."

Together, they carried her back through the kitchen to her bed, put a compress on the wound, and began to pray that she would awaken.

It was hours before the doc arrived, and she still hadn't stirred. The town barber, who also served as undertaker, had removed the bodies of McGregor, the driver, and Smithson, the banker. The Chinese family of One-Eyed George had come for him, and carried him away. The girls had run off the few customers who wanted to stay, and cleaned up the mess. Betsylou's breathing was rapid and sometimes ragged, and her eyes occasionally fluttered, but nothing more.

After Doc Pritchard, who also was a temporary preacher in the Lutheran church until a permanent one could be found, finally examined her, he merely shook his head. He rose and repacked his black bag.

"What?" Helen asked.

"Don't know. I imagine she's got a fractured skull, or at least a terrible concussion. She'll either wake up, or she won't. Nothing to be done other than wait."

Helen stared after him in stunned silence as he pushed his way through the other girls and left.

"I hate that pious son of a bitch," Helen said, then went to get a wet cloth for Betsylou's pale forehead.

The dawn seemed brighter than most, even though some heavy clouds threatened from the west.

Sam was up before light and out with his rifle, trying to replace the meat they'd lost. He moved down to the creek bed and jumped a small whitetail doe. She was barren, so he dropped her with a shot, quickly gutted her, and headed back to camp with her over the back of the grulla behind the saddle, and her heart and liver still steaming in his saddlebags.

The rest of them were up by the time he arrived, and greeted him with a wide smile and a full pot of coffee.

In moments, the women had fresh liver in the frying pan.

"I was worried about taking that shot," Sam said to Silas, "but we had to have something to gnaw on."

"Hell's fire, ol' coon, them old Bloods got more holes in 'em than the last ten-pound round of Limburger I et on. They is heading back up north with they tail between they legs. It's gonna be a cakewalk clear on in to Helena, if'n the weather don't come down on us."

"Hope you're right," Sam said. "I sure hope you're right."

Rusty Pacovsky was eye-to-eye with both Indians, arguing about the whiskey, when they heard a distant shot.

"Now, that there is probably our man. Let's go bushwhack the beggar and then you two can buy your own whiskey. . . . Hell, we get him across the saddle and you can have the bottle in my bedroll with my compliments."

The Crees looked at each other and seemed to accept this as an alternative to drinking Rusty's bottle for breakfast.

They quickly saddled up, and in moments were mounted. They had a short argument as to where the shot had come from; then Rusty settled it. "We'll head back to Deep Creek and pick up the old trading trail, then move up toward the canyon mouth. I'm sure it was from that general direction. Let's ride," and he whipped his horse with the tails of his reins.

In minutes they were back on the trail. Rusty reined up. "Let's ride easy now. We want to see them afore they see us. You can shoot the old woman down if you want, but don't be shootin' the young one. She's mine. Kill the men first." Then he had a second thought. "You two ride on ahead. Give me a sign if you see them, and I'll rein off the trail. They won't get their hackles up if they see a couple of braves. . . . This is the old trading trail."

He let Charley Mad-in-the-Morning ride on ahead, and then Little Ears followed. He stayed a good twenty-five yards behind the other two. If old man McGraw was a little trigger-happy, he wanted the Cree between him and that old man's heavy Sharps. Rusty had seen him shoot.

As they reached a bend in the creek, Little Ears reined up and turned to wave

Rusty up to join them. He gigged his horse, then pulled up beside the Cree. Charley pointed at a little side creek, then up it to where a fine wisp of smoke wormed its way into the sky out from behind a stand of cottonwood. Then he pointed at his nose and whiffed.

Rusty took a long deep inhale and smiled. "Damned if I don't smell something a-fryin'." He laughed out loud and shook his head. "I'd bet a week's wages that's your bottle of whiskey up there in them trees," he said. "I got a plan. You boys wander on into their camp, and while they're busy palaverin' with you, I'll put the sneak up on the high side where I can get a good shot. You be ready when you hear the shootin'."

Both Charley and Little Ears eyed him skeptically.

"Don't be givin' me that evil eye. You want your whiskey, an' your five dollars, you'll do as I say."

They reined away, then moved on up the little creek, away from Deep Creek.

Rusty looked the situation over, then rode on up the creek until he reached a spot where the canyon began in earnest. He gigged the horse up a game trail, heading for a stand of lodgepole where he

205

thought he could find a spot overlooking the camp where the smoke originated.

Sam was just chewing the last bite of his portion of liver, and returning the tin plate to the ladies, who were frying up some for lunch later in the day, when he noticed Silas looking off down the creek. Then Sam noticed a spruce grouse gliding away.

He dropped the plate and returned to the rock where he was sitting, which was still supporting his leaning Winchester. Retrieving it, he moved to where Silas sat.

"What do you see, old man?"

"I see a spooked grouse, and I'm wonderin' what got it up in the air."

In a moment, his question was answered as two riders appeared. The man in the lead, an Indian in grungy leather leggings with a red linsey-woolsey shirt, waved at him. Then the Indian following did also.

"Friendly couple of fellows," Silas said, but his tone was less than friendly.

"Bloods?" Sam asked.

"Cree," Silas said. "You recognize them?"

Sam studied them as they got closer. "I don't think I'll ever forget the pockmarked one. I'd say they were the two with Sheriff Thacker and his bunch."

"Seems like it to me."

Both the Indians had their rifles sheathed in beaded leather scabbards tied to their saddles. Neither wore a side arm, only knives.

Silas gave them a belated wave in return. "We might as well see what they're up to, but keep a sharp eye out. I don't figure 'em to be alone."

Sixteen

The two Crees reined up twenty feet from the fire, and the man in the lead pointed to his nose. "Good smell," he said.

"Liver," Silas said with a smile, as if they were as welcome as a warm summer morning. "You savvy white talk?"

The pockmarked one nodded.

"Then climb on down and have some liver. Man needs a good breakfast to stick to his ribs."

The pockmarked one glanced at his friend, who immediately dismounted and reached to slip his rifle from its sheath.

"Hold on," Silas said, his buffalo gun in hand. "You want breakfast, you don't need no rifle to take advantage of my hospitality."

The taller of the two Indians shrugged and moved on to the fire, leaving his rifle behind. As did the pockmarked one. Talking Woman filled two plates and waved

them at a couple of rocks just right for sitting, but they ignored her and sat cross-
legged on the ground.

Sam yelled at the ladies, his voice rude
and completely unlike any tone he'd ever
taken with them. "You two, get over here
and help me pack."

Mary looked at him oddly, but Talking
Woman seemed to understand. Both of
them gathered things up, including the un-
washed dishes other than the ones the
Cree were using, and moved among the
horses.

Sam ambled over to the big grulla stud
and stood between it and Silas's paint.
When he had the chance, he spoke to the
ladies quietly. "Something's not right.
Those are the Cree who were with
Thacker back at your old camp." Both of
the ladies nodded, as they were well aware
of the fact. "I'm gonna ride out, just in
case the rest of them are out in the bushes.
No sense in bringing this down on your
family."

"We fight with you, Sam," Talking
Woman said, "as you fought with us." It
was the longest sentence Sam had ever
heard her say. She pointed at the small
pistol she had hidden up the billowing
sleeve of the blouse she now wore.

Sam gave her a quick smile, but shook his head. "Don't want any of you hurt on my account."

He had only loosened Blue's cinch when he'd come in from hunting, and now he quickly retightened it. Then in one swinging motion, he was astride. As he mounted, he saw a flash of reflected sun in the pines above their camp, a hundred or so yards away.

He gave his heels to Blue, and the big stud kicked up sand behind him and charged right through the middle of the camp, making the Crees scatter.

"Take cover, someone's up on the mountain," Sam yelled, crashing across the little creek and up the hill. The creek made a bend to the east above their camp, where a ravine had been cut into the steep mountain behind them.

Behind him, the Crees started to stand, but Silas waved them back down with the Sharps. "Y'all jus' sit there and enjoy yer breakfast." He took the caution of stepping back a few paces so he was behind a large cottonwood but still had a clear view of the Cree.

Staring at the .50-caliber muzzle of the big gun, they did as they were told.

Sam, fifty yards up the mountain,

ducked low in the saddle just as a tongue of fire showed the location of a shooter in the woods above. He felt the slap of wind from a passing bullet and heard the muzzle blast.

Jerking rein, he worked the grulla first left, then right, zigzagging up the mountain, away from the camp, closer to his attacker.

How many were up there? It had been four white men and the two Indian trackers when he'd had his run-in down on the Yellowstone, and he presumed the same at the McGraws' camp. Had they all followed him this far?

One thing was sure, he didn't want to bring this down on the McGraws. But it looked as if he already had.

The pines clawed at his face and chest, and then another shot rang out from above. But he was rapidly closing the gap between himself and the shooters.

Sam drew the Remington revolver when he thought he was very close, and as he did so, a man rose up out of the brush twenty yards in front of him and brought his rifle sights down on Sam's chest. Blue, as if on cue, shied to the left and stumbled on a rock pile, going to his knees and almost somersaulting.

Sam flew over the stud's head but hit rolling, then threw himself to his stomach and levered back the revolver that he'd managed to hang on to. The big horse struggled to his feet, losing purchase in the shale and stumbling back down the mountain as he did so, then recovering and trotting off into the brush.

Sam could not see the man who'd appeared in front of him, but that was probably a good thing, as the man surely could not see him. He lay silent for a moment, then crabbed to the protection of a large lodgepole and situated himself under its low boughs. All was silent.

In a moment, he could hear Silas yelling orders at the two Indians down below. Relieved, Sam figured old Silas would have things well in hand back in the camp.

Sam waited for what he thought was an eternity, then picked up a rock and chucked it back down the mountain the way he'd come, and as soon as he turned back the man rose up and fired in the direction of the noise Sam had made.

Sam squeezed off a shot from the revolver, as his rifle was still on the saddle. The man jerked backward out of sight.

Again, Sam waited, and waited. He heard some shuffling movement in the underbrush above, but nothing more.

Until, finally, a shaky voice rang out, "Hey, you . . . Stranahan. I'm hit bad. I need help here."

Still, Sam waited. The som'bitch knew his name, so this was a posse of some sort. He'd been surprised when he'd heard no more shooting from other sources. Could it be that it was just this man and the Cree?

Finally, he moved away from his spot and worked his way up the mountain until he was above the last spot he'd seen the man. Then he remembered, he'd caught a flash of red hair. Hell, he was not only known by the shooter, but he knew him. Rusty somebody. The old boy sure carried a grudge. Finally, the voice rang out again.

"Hey there, Stranahan. I'm gonna bleed out, if'n you don't come help me. You want a dead lawman on your hands?"

Sam worked his way toward the voice until he figured he was no more than thirty feet from the spot.

"Throw out your weapon, and I'll give you a hand."

"You won't shoot me down?"

"You mean like you tried to shoot me down?"

"Goldang, Stranahan, you're a wanted man."

"Throw out your gun."

In a second, a Winchester flew out over some brush.

"Now your side arm."

"Don't carry one."

"No side arm comes out of there, no help."

"Goldang, this hurts like the devil."

"No sidearm, no help."

In less than another second, a heavy revolver came sailing out over the brush.

"Now stand up," Sam instructed.

"Hell, I can't stand up. I'm shot bad."

"You got another gun you'll be shot a lot worse."

"I got a pocketknife is all. Now come help me."

Sam worked his way down to almost where he thought Rusty was, then threw another rock to the far side of the man. But nothing this time.

He peeked over the brush, and Pacovsky eyed him, then lay back, one hand high on his chest, blood seeping between his fingers.

"You done shot me good. Can't get this damn hole to stop pumpin' blood," he said.

Sam moved over to him, then, satisfied he had no weapon, shoved his own revolver back in its holster. Jerking Rusty's shirt out of where it was stuffed in his pants, he tore away some strips. He stuffed the wound with the cloth and tied more strips around his shoulder and his chest, binding the stuffed cloth into the puckered hole. By the time he was finished, Rusty only had half a shirt left.

"That'll hold you until we can get Talking Woman to take a look at it. She'll have something —"

"Ain't no bloody heathen gonna tend me."

"Then go ahead and bleed to death. Tell the truth, I don't much give a damn."

"You got me, but you won't get far. You're a wanted man."

"I may be, but I sure as hell didn't do anything to warrant it."

Parovsky moaned and winced. Then muttered, "I know you didn't. . . ." He started to say something, then bit his tongue, before he continued in a more demanding tone, "And I don't give a damn. Somebody, even if it ain't me, somebody is gonna collect five hundred dollars for your ugly hide."

Sam started to move away to fetch Blue,

then realized what the man had said. "What do you mean, you know I didn't do anything?"

"I didn't say that."

"The hell you didn't. I'm gonna unwrap you and let you bleed out, right here, if you don't spit it out."

"No, no, don't do that. I need a doctor."

"You need to tell me what you know, and you need to do it damned fast before I leave you here for the buzzards."

"A doctor?"

"No doctor, until I think you've told me all you know about why I'm being hunted by Thacker."

Rusty was quiet for a moment, then looked down at the hand that had been holding his shoulder. Blood again seeped through his fingers. He glared at Sam. "You tell I tolt, and I'll call you a bloody liar."

"Just tell me what the hell is up."

"Thacker, he was behind robbin' the stage."

"What stage?"

"The Overland, the day before we found your camp down on the Yellowstone. We was actin' like we was huntin' robbers, but we damn well knew who done it, 'cause it was . . . it was some of Thacker's men.

216

Thacker's men and some fellows named Hutchins and Pendergast. They done it, and we was just making it look good doing the posse." He moaned and winced, then spoke through clenched teeth. "Get me to a doctor."

"I'll get you back to camp, and then Mrs. McGraw will tend you. Then you can go back and tell your sheriff that I won't be runnin' anywhere other than to Bozeman, should I find out I'm still a wanted man. I'll march his fat ass down Main Street with his pants draggin' again, should he not put this right. If he doesn't, by all that's holy, I'll put a forty-four right in that big butt of his."

"I'll tell him, now get me down there. Even that Blackfeet woman will do. I believe I'm dyin'."

"I doubt it. Montana Territory couldn't be so lucky, but I'll get you down there." Sam stomped away, hunting for the grulla.

At midmorning, Miss Betsylou Maddigan stopped breathing.

She passed peaceably, but that fact didn't quell the crying and sobbing that went on in her establishment for some hours afterward. Many of the girls wailed not only for Betsylou, but for their doubts

217

as to what their future held.

Marshal Clark Peckham showed up in the early afternoon, and took statements from each of them, regarding what had happened and who was in attendance. Since he had taken office two years before, Phillipsburg had only had five killings, and four of them had been in the last few days. It had been a busy week, and might become even busier.

In fact the coming few days might just be a real challenge, if any of the rumblings about town that morning came to fruition. He'd been warned by several that the general feeling was that there was no reason to wait for Circuit Judge Horace Talbot to get around to coming to Phillipsburg. The populace seemed to think they could take care of the problem of Tucker Stark themselves. A short trial, a vote of that portion of the general populace gathered in the street, and then a hanging from whatever cross beam might be high enough would do just fine for Tucker Stark, whether the marshal approved or not.

McGregor and Smithson had been well-liked and well-respected townsmen, and even One-Eyed George Choi had his friends. And though it wouldn't be readily admitted, Miss Betsylou Maddigan had her admirers among a certain gender around town.

Peckham had no interest in a lynching taking place in his town, and let any who would listen know that fact.

But letting them know, and stopping them, might be two different things.

When Sam returned to camp, with Rusty Pacovsky in the grulla's saddle and him afoot, Silas and the ladies had the two Crees bound back to back. Neither of them had quite finished his breakfast, and both of them looked as if they had indigestion.

Talking Woman sent Mary on a quest to find some herbs that she used to dress Rusty Pacovsky's wounds. Then he was bound also.

While this was going on, Sam took the two Indian rifles out of their scabbards and pounded the firing pins flat, then went back up the mountain and did the same to Rusty Pacovsky's rifle and handgun.

"Weren't no reason to do that," Pacovsky said when Sam returned and threw the redhead's weapons in a pile with those of the Cree. "What if we come upon some renegade Blackfeet?"

"You done did," Silas said, and guffawed. For the first time since he'd met her, Talking Woman laughed aloud.

Sam eyeballed Rusty Pacovsky, then snarled, "Oh, like you wouldn't be back-shootin' us as we rode away." He laughed at Rusty's foolishness.

"No, I wouldn't," Pacovsky said.

Sam shook his head. "You know, Pacovsky, a fella can go to hell for looking another fella right in the eye and lying like that. You three can make it back to Bozeman with a little luck." Then on second thought, Sam added, "Don't you die on the way, Pacovsky. I may need someone to tell the judge what you told me."

"I ain't gonna die," he said, and spat on the ground.

This time Sam smiled, not at what the redhead had said, but what he didn't. What he didn't say was that he, sure as the hubs of hell were hard, wouldn't go out of his way to testify for old Sam Stranahan. *Well*, Sam thought, *I'll cross that bridge when I come to it. At least now I know what tom-foolery is going on down in Bozeman.*

They rode out for Helena, freeing Rusty Pacovsky and leaving him to try and untie the Cree with one good arm, and the Cree to figure out how to get the wounded man back to Bozeman.

Sam again smiled, but this time at the thought of Pacovsky bouncing along on a travois, wincing with every rock it was dragged over.

Seventeen

The next morning dawned with a sky as flat and gray as a granite tabletop.

Four funerals were scheduled that day. Two at the Phillipsburg cemetery and two at the nearby county plots. Smithson, the banker, would be buried first, then McGregor, so those that wanted could stay for his planting. Both Miss Betsylou Maddigan and One-Eyed George Choi could afford to be buried at the Phillipsburg cemetery, on the north side of town up beyond Clark Street, but the general populace would not hear of the Chinaman being buried there, and the female population would not condone Betsylou having a place so near that of their relatives, or maybe someday, even themselves.

It was suspected that Smithson's would be by far the best attended, but all were surprised to find that McGregor drew even more folks. While Smithson had those dressed in city finery, McGregor's attracted most of those folks, plus miners and cattlemen, freighters and laborers, and even most of the town's drunks. He was a well-liked Scotsman, one of the best in Montana Territory with the traces and a four-up, and had the reputation of being generous far beyond most of those with his heritage.

To the great surprise of many, One-Eyed George drew the second largest crowd. Some may have been there only out of curiosity, to see the city's few dozen Chinese in their mourning garb of all white, as opposed to the city folk dressed generally in black, and to view the celebration that both proceeded and followed. The procession carrying George's body wound its way out of town with participants flying paper dragons and other effigies, and Chinese drums being beaten. It was good it was the last funeral of the day, as it would have been impossible to have heard the preacher at the nearby Phillipsburg cemetery, should the funerals have taken place at the same time.

Betsylou's funeral boasted only a few, all of the girls and a few single men, most of whom hoped they wouldn't be seen by the townspeople. Marshal Clark Peckham was the only one who boldly rode up on his horse, directly from town, and rode directly back after the words were said. Doc Pritchard, the acting minister, did not attend.

What words were read were read by Miss Helen.

But for all the people at all three other funerals, the most tears were shed at Betsylou's.

The trip on down Deep Creek to the Missouri was uneventful. Only twenty miles or so south of where they found the north-flowing river it was formed by the confluence of the Madison, the Jefferson, and the Gallatin. Then it began its trip to St. Louis where it mingled its waters with the Mississippi, then on to New Orleans. When they crossed the river, it would be only a day and a half's ride to Helena . . . if they could cross. As it was, they had to turn south for a few miles, as the river ran cold and deep, and Silas wouldn't try it with the ladies. A decision Sam thought wise.

Only another two days then. He could wait two days to find his brother, Liam.

Juston Crossing was the site of a small trading post and a flatboat ferry, and by pushing hard they arrived there in the early afternoon. The trading post was a simple structure, a rectangular log building with a single window of waxed paper on each end, and a doorway facing the river. Beyond it was a small cabin, with its chimney roiling smoke into the gray sky. Between the two a small privy offered access from both the cabin and the trading post.

Sam had a pocketful of money, and was anxious to stand Silas to a drink and the ladies to whatever pleased them. They tied the stock on the hitching rail outside the plank door, as the ferry was across the river, picking up some travelers.

A woman as tall as Silas, and as broad as Blue's backside, moved behind a plank bar as they came in.

As Sam grew closer, he could see that she could have used some grooming. She had a wart on her cheekbone the size of the end of his index finger, and it had a spray of black hairs an inch long growing out of it. She was missing a few front teeth, and her face was blotched with red marks — Sam presumed they came from the consumption of some of her own goods.

But she was a happy sort. "Howdy, howdy, welcome to Juston's Crossing. . . .

I'm Mrs. Juston. We got Miner's Gulch Beer, fresh from Helena, we got root beer, we got flour and baking soda, and all the fixin's, including tobacco twists and smoke. Now, let me tell you, we got some of the finest whiskey in all the Montana Territory. What'll it be?"

Sam moved to the end of the twelve-foot planks that served as the bar, and smiled at her. "Give us two whiskeys, and give the ladies whatever they want."

Her look soured when it appeared she first realized that the ladies were Blackfeet. "Ask 'em to come over here and sit up to the bar. I don't want 'em shuffling through my goods."

Sam was tempted to tell her to put her goods where the sun didn't shine, but she was a woman, no matter what her size and looks, and he thought better of it when Silas merely ignored her.

"Whatever they find that they fancy, I'll be buyin' for them."

She looked him up and down; then a shocked expression covered her broad face. "Why, you're . . . Why, that's fine," she said, and turned to pour the drinks.

Sam glanced to his right, and was face-to-face with his image staring back at him, and the big bold sign, $500.00 REWARD.

He was shown as a rugged sort, with shoulder-length hair, which he guessed he had. And a stubble of beard, which he damn well knew he had.

He motioned to Silas and pointed to the handbill. Before Silas could comment, the woman turned back with the whiskey.

"That'll be fifty cents," she said, all joviality gone from her voice.

Sam slapped a five-dollar gold piece on the bar, then called out to Mary and Talking Woman, "What can I get you ladies to drink?"

Both of them turned and shook their heads. They seemed far too involved with several bolts of cloth. Mary held up a gingham of bright red across her bosom, and smiled at her mother.

"How much for that?" Sam asked.

"Ten cents a yard, or two dollars for the whole bolt," the woman said, never taking her eyes off the ladies.

"Then give me my two and a half dollars' change."

Only then did she turn back, and a smile crossed her face. "You want the whole bolt?"

"You said two dollars. You owe me two dollars and fifty cents' change."

She fished out the money and shoved it

across the bar, as he threw the three fingers of rye to the back of his throat with one sweep.

"I've got to go out and meet the ferry," she said.

Sam was a little surprised that she was willing to leave them inside with her precious goods, then realized she might have motive to her madness.

"I think you better stay here in case the ladies want something more. I'll go out and help the ferry master."

"That's my husband —" She started for the door.

Sam blocked her way. "I said, you stay here." His tone was as hard as the cast-iron potbellied stove that rested in a corner of the room.

Her face flashed a little fear, and she backed away. "All right, mister. Whatever you say."

Sam moved on outside, and saw that the ferry was three-quarters of the way back. And to his dismay, he saw that it carried a half dozen mounted bluecoats. Each wore a side arm and carried a Springfield .45/70 carbine in a saddle sheath.

Sam decided he had no choice other than to play it quiet and act as if he worked there. If they'd seen the handbill, he'd be looking down the muzzles of a half dozen weapons.

As the ferry bumped against the landing, he smiled and waved. "Howdy, howdy, welcome to Juston's Crossing. We got beer and whiskey inside."

The ferry master cast him a quizzical glance, but didn't question his good fortune at having someone there to help him dock.

"The Second Cavalry's been here many times, son," an old grizzled sergeant growled. "We got no time. Form up, ride by twos," he yelled at his men, and mounted up and moved on away from the landing.

Hardly giving him a sideways glance, the others mounted and followed. The sarge must have been a hard taskmaster, as the troops were a fine-looking bunch: McClellan saddles were well oiled, each wore a cartridge belt of the latest design rather than carrying a cartridge box, they sported matching campaign hats all of which were black, their blue blouses were buttoned, and all wore corduroy trousers that had been gleaming white at one time neatly tucked into black troop boots. Had Sam seen them in a parade, he couldn't have imagined a finer-looking bunch.

The ferry master was a bear of a man, with a face and body as wide as his wife's, but he stood a good foot taller. Far taller than Sam.

"Thanks for the help, stranger."

Then he took a step closer and studied Sam, who started moving away. "Ain't I seen you somewhere before? Helena maybe?"

"No," Sam said. "Just rode in from Wyoming."

The man started to follow Sam up to the trading post, but Sam stopped and turned back to him. "I got three more horsebackers with me. We want to cross, now."

The big man sighed. "Sure enough. Fetch 'em out if you got the dollar. . . . It's two bits apiece. But hurry it up, I still ain't had my dinner."

"We'll be right there."

Sam walked to the door and yelled at the others to come on. When they got to the ferry, the master was fiddling with his lines.

The woman stuck her head out the door and yelled at him, "Everett, you get on up here for a minute."

He started to move off the ferry, but Sam stopped him. "We're in a mite of a hurry, neighbor. You take us across right now, or I will, and you'll be shy a green-back."

"And how the hell am I supposed to get my ferry back?"

"I'd suggest you ride along."

He glared at Sam a moment, then poled the flatboat away from the bank.

"Everett, you get up here, right this minute."

But he paid little attention to her.

"You a married man?" the big man asked Sam.

"No, sir," he said, and couldn't help glancing at Miss Mary.

"Good thing. You don't seem to have the temperament for it," he said, then began to whistle, then halfway across, to sing.

On the other side of the river, they watched the ferry pole away on its way back to the trading post, and then Sam spoke to Silas as they mounted up. "That wasn't a good situation. Pretty damn good likeness on that handbill, and a patrol of bluecoats. Good thing they seemed to be in such a hurry."

"Sure enough," Silas said, and grinned. "They probably had pay waitin' at Fort Ellis. We got to find you a barber in Helena and lower your ears and scrape that beard off."

"Sounds right to me."

They gigged the horses, and set off at a lope for Helena, the territorial capital. Now that they were enjoying the Fort Ellis to Helena Road, the going was much easier.

The problem was, if there was a handbill at Juston's Crossing, truly a one-horse town, then how many handbills were there in Helena?

He turned to Silas, who was again afoot. "I thought you said you were off to the Flint Mountains, or maybe the Hellgate country."

"Maybe, in a bit. But we're gonna ride into Helena with you, ol' coon, and make sure y'all get that shave and trim afore some old law dog bolts the irons on you."

"Not necessary, Silas, as much as I enjoy the McGraws' company."

"Weren't necessary for you to get amidst our squabble with Hunting Hawk. . . ." He stepped up his pace. "In a few hours, we'll be in Helena, drinking good whiskey with your kin in Last Chance Gulch."

"It's your decision," Sam said.

Then he glanced back at Mary and smiled, and got a blush in return.

He turned his attention back to Silas. "I think it was someplace called Grizzly Gap, where Liam has his diggin's."

"That's twixt Helena and Unionville . . . or maybe Park City. Not far out of Helena. No hill for a stepper."

Sam smiled. It had been the better part of ten years since he'd seen Liam. He could hardly wait.

Eighteen

Miss Helen had decided that she would no longer use the name, and now let all the girls know she was to be known as Miss Maureen O'Toole, of county Cork, Ireland, and proud of it.

The bank had been closed the day after the funeral, but had reopened under the direction of — to most of the town's great chagrin — young Billy Smithson, the twenty-two-year-old son of William Smithson Sr. The young bank president had already suffered the withdrawal of a half dozen accounts that morning.

Maureen had just come from Parker Willingham at the express company, and had the will in hand. She wore a prim and proper yellow gown, with a fashionable bustle, and carried a yellow and red parasol. The reticule she carried was also tied in yellow and red, as was her sable hair with the same colored ribbon. Had one not known better she would have appeared to be the recently demised banker's wife, or a townswoman of considerable standing.

Striding in boldly she crossed the small lobby, passed the tellers' cages, and pushed through a little swinging gate of walnut stained turned posts, then walked to the banker's desk. "Do you have a minute?"

"Surely," the young man said, rolling his sleeves back down and grabbing his coat off a coat stand near his desk. He put it on, shot his sleeves out, adjusted his wire spectacles, and motioned for her to take a seat across from him.

She did so, and spread the will out on the desk in front of him. "I'm Miss Maureen O'Toole, and I'm sorry for your loss, Mr. Smithson. Your father was a fine man and a gentleman."

"Thank you." He looked at her over his half glasses, wondering how valuable the compliment was, coming from a soiled dove. "Now what can I do for you?"

"You can see by that document, Liam Stranahan's last will and testament, that I'm a partial owner in the Siglinda One and Two. I want you to keep this in your vault for me."

The young man cleared his throat. "Are you a customer of the bank, Miss O'Toole?"

"If you'll have me as one." She picked up her reticule and pulled a cloth bag out that took up almost all the space in the small purse. "Here's three thousand dollars, mostly in gold coin, but some scrip, that I'd like to deposit."

Billy Smithson was a young man, but no fool. He gave her a tight smile. "Then I'd say you're a customer, Miss O'Toole, and I'm pleased to welcome you to Miner's and Merchant's."

"It's my understanding the bank holds a small mortgage on Miss Betsylou Maddigan's house up on the hill."

"That's right. Did she share that information with you?"

"She did. In fact, she shared everything with me. I know she had a small account here at the bank, and a mortgage that she could have paid off at any time . . . but she wanted your father's goodwill, and he was . . . He often visited. Betsylou and I were very good friends. And as you may know, Miss Maddigan has no heirs, and left no will."

"No heirs so far as we *know*. It'll take some time to settle the estate, and we are very concerned that somewhere someone may lay claim to the house and the small account she maintained here. If not, she

236

died intestate, and her estate will escheat to the territory."

"And in the meantime?"

"What do you propose?"

Maureen sat up straight and prim in the chair. "I propose that I continue to make payments on the mortgage, and continue to occupy the house with the other girls. All of them have consented to work for me."

"Rental on the house would be much more than the small payments on the mortgage, Miss O'Toole. I will probably be appointed executor of the estate, as my father was for so many over the years, and I have a fiduciary responsibility to the estate. I'd suggest you pay a fair rental on the house, out of which the payments will be taken, and the rest will go into her account to be held for . . . for whomever."

"And what would that rental be?"

"It's probably worth as much as thirty-five dollars a month."

"To someone maybe," she said, and smiled tightly at him.

"But you can stay on for thirty."

"I think it's probably worth thirty. It's a fine house, but I can move elsewhere for half that. So I think twenty would be overly generous."

"Twenty-seven fifty."

"Twenty-five, or I'll take that sack of money back and buy the best house in town."

He cleared his throat, and smiled. "Twenty-five it is, and it's been a pleasure doing business with you."

She rose. "I hope we'll do a lot more business, Mr. Smithson."

"Come back any time," he said, picking up the sack of money so she wouldn't be tempted to do exactly as she said.

"A deposit slip for the money, please, and a receipt for the will, stating the general terms, if you would be so kind."

He smiled, sat, and picked up a pen and sheet of foolscap.

Just about an hour before sunset, Sam reined Blue up on a small rise just east of Helena. As they'd neared the capital, they'd encountered more and more traffic on the road. Each wagon or rider he'd viewed with some worry, but none had given him more than a passing glance.

The view in front of him was impressive. From the time gold was discovered in '64, the town had continued to grow. It now featured a number of fine brick buildings fanning out from Last Chance Gulch, where the original discoveries were made, and boasted a population of over four thousand, with at least a couple of church spires visible.

Sam was anxious, but not so anxious he wanted to shoot it out with some innocent lawman just trying to do his job. As Rusty Pacovsky had pointed out, he didn't want to kill a lawman . . . any more than he wanted to be killed by one. "Why don't you folks go on into town? I think I'll wait till dark."

Silas nodded. "Sure 'nuff. That handbill back there did spook you some, didn't it?"

"I don't want trouble. I just want to find my brother."

"I'll be askin' around. There's a waterin' hole down on the street west of Last Chance Gulch. I'm thinkin' it's Park Avenue, or some such. Place was called the Last Chance Saloon the last time I meandered through. I'll be there come six o'clock, and be a-waitin' for you."

"I'll come in, soon as it's good and dark."

Sam rode off the road and found a grassy spot to graze the grulla. The mountains in the far distance were crowned with white, but the ground here was clean of snow, with only the occasional patch visible up in the nearby hills, and those in the shady spots.

When it was good and dark he let Blue set his own pace, and in twenty minutes reined up in front of the Last Chance. It was a two-story wood affair, with a false front and a large several-paned window facing the cobbled street. He tied the grulla next to a paint horse he recognized as Silas's and went to the swinging doors and gave the interior a good looking over before he pushed through. There were no lawmen in the place, at least no badges he could see.

A couple of faro games were well attended, and a wheel of chance had a table full of eager and noisy players. Near the front doors, just inside a window, a stocky bald-headed fellow who seemed to be all knuckles banged away on an upright piano. Chopin was *not* the composer of choice. One of the pieces he seemed to be hitting all around was right out of the recent unpleasantries, and sounded like it should have stayed on the battlefield.

Silas stood at the bar talking with another old-timer with a beard equal to Silas's, and who looked as if he'd prospected every square foot from California to Montana. Sam walked to the end of the bar where he had no competition for the bartender's attention, and waved him over. "Two whiskeys, please," he said, and the man glanced at him, but didn't seem to think it unusual.

As soon as Silas saw him, he tipped his hat at the fella he'd been talking with, and rounded the end of the bar to join Sam. "That fer me?" he asked, motioning at the second whiskey.

"That it is. What did you find out?"

"Beer's right good here to wash it down with."

Sam waved the bartender back over, and ordered a couple of beers.

"You were right," Silas offered. "Your brother had a claim up in Grizzly Gulch."

"Had?"

"He sold out, and him and a friend lit out for Phillipsburg."

"How far's that?"

"Fifty miles as the crow flies. Two and a half days of hard riding, since we ain't crows. Good road, the Mullen Trail, all the way to Deer Creek; then we cut off and head up 'round the Flint Range."

"I'll leave tomorrow."

"No, we'll leave tomorrow. Like I tolt you, Flint Creek is one of the hidey-holes where I like to winter up. Was good

241

trappin' in some of the side cricks and canyons, and plenty of elk and deer in the hills . . . so we'll be ridin' along, if'n it suits you."

"Not only suits me, but pleases me, Silas. Where did you deposit the ladies?"

"Just outside of town. Made camp on Prickly Pear Creek, just after we left you. Surprised you didn't see 'em."

"I saw a campfire, but I was headin' on in to meet you. You ready to head back out there?"

"That rye is sitting pretty easy in my ol' gut. Maybe after a couple more, if'n you got the wherewithall."

"My pleasure, but I don't want to leave the ladies alone there for long."

Silas glowered at that. "You seem to be gettin' right attached to my womenfolk."

He was giving Sam the evil eye, but then broke into a grin, then guffawed loudly as Sam colored a little.

"Damned old fool," Sam said, just before he took a long draw on the beer the bartender had brought, and Silas slapped him on the back, splashing the beer over his cheeks.

Sam fished out a towel hanging on a hook under the bar, and wiped his mouth, as Silas laughed even harder.

But they only finished that one round as a town marshal, with his copper badge plain as day on his lapel, came in with a couple of range hands.

Sam and Silas bottomed up both beers and whiskies, and left.

Later, as he rolled up in the buffalo robe near the campfire the ladies had built, Sam had no remorse for not being in Helena longer. No remorse except of course that he hadn't yet found Liam. And hadn't found a barber.

Rusty Pacovsky finally rode into Bozeman.

The Cree had immediately dug out the bottle when he'd cut them loose, and had gotten falling-down drunk, then refused to leave the next day as they were badly affected with the bottle ailment. There wasn't a damn thing he'd been able to do about it, but wait, and hurt.

Pacovsky reined up in front of the sheriff's office and clumsily dismounted. The sling he wore was woefully inadequate, and his shoulder had seeped blood most of the way back to Bozeman. It streaked his shirt past his belt to his trousers.

Sheriff Hiram Thacker filled the doorway before Pacovsky could cross the boardwalk. "What the hell! I guess you don't have him, since you seem to be shot all to hell, and I don't see him draped across no horse."

"I found him, but I don't got him."

"So, did he get ripe on ya? Is he buried out there somewheres?"

"Nope, not unless he fell off'n his horse and broke his fool neck after he got away, and that prairie scum piled rock on him somewheres."

Thacker shook his head. Had Rusty not already been shot, he was mad enough to shoot him himself. "Well, damn your worthless hide. Damn your shot-up worthless hide. Now the judge is gonna chew my cherries. Go on in and lie down in one of the cells, and I'll go fetch the doc. If I hang around here, I'd probably lock the damn door and just let you rot."

As he turned to leave to find the doctor, Judge Horace Talbot was crossing the muddy street with a pronounced limp — his gout flaring up again. As he closed the distance, Pacovsky did as suggested and walked in and through to the jail cells.

"Was that Pacovsky?" the judge asked.

"Yes, sir." And before the judge could ask, he added, "And never send somebody else to do what you should be doing yourself."

"What you're paid to do, I might add."

Thacker sighed deeply. "I know, I know. I'll get a posse together and go after the som'bitch myself . . . O'course, the handbills will probably work a lot cheaper than some posse."

"I've got to take the stage over to Phillipsburg in the morning. You do as you see fit."

"You got a trial?"

"Shouldn't take long. Some fella shot down the town banker, a stage driver, a Chinaman, and beat a sporting woman to death, all in front of about two dozen credible witnesses. Like I say, shouldn't take long."

"We should have him by the time you get back."

The judge chuckled sarcastically. "If past performance is any example, I won't hold my breath, Hiram."

"I got to go find the doc for Pacovsky." He started to walk away.

"Did this Stranahan shoot him, or did he fall off his horse? I saw he was bound up."

"He did shoot him."

"Then we can add another charge . . . assaulting an officer, or maybe attempted murder, depending upon the circumstances. You get it all documented while I'm gone."

As Thacker walked away, he waved over his shoulder, and offered in a voice that diminished as he moved away, "Hell, we got a hanging charge on him now. I wouldn't waste the paperwork."

"Humph," the judge said, then turned and started limping to his hotel room to pack.

It was a long, muddy, bouncy ride to Phillipsburg.

And far worse than normal when your gout was giving you the devil, and every jiggle of the stage was like turning a knife in your gut.

With any luck, he'd get this fellow Stark hung in record time, and be on his way back to Bozeman.

Nineteen

Gunter Kauffmann waited until he was completely out of supplies before he chanced going back into Phillipsburg. But he now had to have them, as well as hire some help.

His first stop was the Phillipsburg Mercantile; then he was going to the Kaiser for a steak and a dozen oysters, then and only then, to Clark Peckham's office. With any luck, Peckham wouldn't be in, but he had told him he would call on him the next time he came to town, and it would look suspicious if he didn't.

To his chagrin, Peckham was at his desk when Gunter ambled in. "You asked me to drop by, Marshal."

"I did. Have a seat, Kauffmann. Coffee?"

"No, I haf dinner just now."

"You had any other thoughts about who killed your partner?"

"Hell no."

"When Vandermer was cleaning out his livery he found some blood we hadn't noticed. Liam's gun had a shell missing. Looks like he got a shot off at the man who gunned him down. You got any holes in you, Kauffmann?"

Gunter laughed aloud. "You come to see me right after da shootin', Peckham. Did you see any hole in me den?"

"Not that I could see, Gunter."

"An' you see me limpin' or goin' to see the doc?"

"No, but that don't mean you wasn't winged."

"You check my shotgun, an' you know it ain't been shot. I tink it time you go lookin' for who did dis ting and leave me be."

Peckham rose, and Kauffmann followed suit. "I'm going to find whoever did this, Gunter."

"I hope so, Marshal." Kauffmann turned and headed for the door.

"By the way, Gunter, you knew Liam left a will?"

Kauffmann stopped in his tracks, and turned slowly back to face Peckham.

"No, I didn't know. What did this will say?"

"It said he left half of his one-half interest to his brother, Sam, and the other portion to Miss Helen, who it turns out is named Maureen O'Toole."

"Miss Helen, up at Betsylou's?"

"One and the same. You got two new partners."

Gunter spun on his heel and stomped out, slamming the door behind him.

It took Sam and the McGraws the better part of three days to reach Phillipsburg. They'd ridden clear of most of the towns on the way, except for Butte, where a silver strike was roaring strong. And they'd only stopped there long enough for Silas to ride in and get some supplies. Sam and the ladies stayed well shy of the bustling little town. The day after that the wind had come up and it was hard riding, crossing the Deer Lodge Valley. When they'd finally reached the protection of the Flint Range, the weather softened.

It was late afternoon of the third day since leaving Helena when they found a nice spot down near Flint Creek and made camp. There was more snow here, the ground lay covered by at least two inches, and the sky to the west looked as if more was to come soon. Even so, it was a pastoral scene. A few homesteads, three or four, dotted the valley to the west of

Phillipsburg, and a few dozen cattle pawed at the shallow snow cover to expose the rich grass of the valley floor.

While they gathered firewood, Sam sidled up to Silas. "I hate to ask you again, but you think you might go into town and see what you can learn? This time, I have no idea where Liam might be."

"I'll see if they's any handbills stuck about."

"Hell, on second thought, I'll go in with you. I'm tired of fightin' shy of those damn handbills, and I got a real itch to find my brother. And I need to find a barber before things close up . . . and before I get locked up."

"Then let's go. I heared last year that they was gonna build a fine hotel, the Kaiser, and maybe it's been done. They had the foundation stones laid last time I was here. Let's go have a whiskey. . . . Hell, it's time I found Miss Mary a husband. Maybe I can pawn the little nubbins off on one of those rich miners."

Sam stiffened. "You don't need to pawn Miss Mary off on any miner."

"Oh, you don't say. You know some reason why I shouldn't? Hell, I might even get one hell of a dowry for the lass, should some mud grubber still have a bit of color in his pouch."

He had a half smile behind the white beard, and a mischievous look in his eye. Sam smiled, and spoke so low the ladies couldn't hear. "Hell, Silas, I'd give you ten quarts of good whiskey. How you gonna beat that?"

Old Silas slapped his thighs and did a little jig. Then he stopped suddenly and gave Sam a hard look. "Hell, boy, I'd let you have her hand for a wink and a hand-shake . . . and a promise you'd treat her good."

Sam turned serious also. "Silas, I'd never treat her any other way . . . but this is all just spittin' in the wind, until I set things straight with the law. When that happens, then you and I'll have a talk."

Silas smiled, then started off on foot, his preferred mode of transportation. Phillips-burg was only a little over a mile to the northeast. Sam mounted up, and followed.

They moved boldly up the middle of Broadway, riding right past Marshal Clark Peckham's office. Sam felt a bolt of heat travel up his backbone when he recognized the handbill plainly displayed next to the marshal's office door, along with a pair of others. Then he noticed a man watching him through the office window as he

251

passed. The man rose and walked a couple of steps until he was almost against the window. Sam slouched in the saddle, and looked the other way. But the man did not come crashing through the door, as Sam feared he might.

In the next block, Sam spotted the painted red and white spiraled pole of the barber. He dismounted and handed Blue's reins to Silas. "Tie ol' Blue outside the Kaiser. I'll join you after I get spiffed up." He watched his rifle move away on the saddle, and wondered if he should have taken it. But Silas would watch it, and Sam had the Remington on his hip.

A small sign over the door read: TON-SORIAL PALACE, UNDERTAKING SER-VICE, AND DENTISTRY. HOT BATHS IN THE REAR.

Sam entered and, being the only one there other than one who must have been the barber, took a seat in the fine oak-and-leather tilt-back barber's chair, as the well-coiffed man in the rear laid down a *Leslie's Weekly* and walked over. "The works?" he asked.

"How much?" Sam asked, as if it made much difference.

"Two bits for the hair and a shave, and a splash of lilac or rose water. You'll smell good as Mrs. Vanderbilt's pet pig."

"Sounds right. Cut it short just so the comb will lay it down, leave the side chops just below the ear."

The barber chuckled. "You're a picky sort, for one who looks like he's been riding all the way from the Chicago stockyards. You can hang that gun belt on a hook over there, and you'll sit a little easier."

"No, thanks. You got a bath in the back?"

"Sign says so, if you read. And don't mind takin' a bath in a room that sometimes doubles as an undertakin' parlor."

"I read, and I got the quarter if you got hot water."

As the barber spoke, he fetched a towel from a pile on a shelf behind the chair, and dropped it in a bucket on top a little potbellied stove. He stropped a razor and laid it aside, then picked up a pair of scissors and went to work on the hair.

"You know a fellow name of Liam Stranahan?" Sam asked the man.

The barber stopped his cutting. "Why do you ask?"

"I need to locate him."

The barber continued trimming. "You got business with Liam?"

"Personal business."

"It's a little late for any kind of business with Liam, friend."

Sam leaned forward, out from under the scissors, and turned so he could see the man. "What does that mean?"

"Poor Liam was shot down more'n a week ago. A fine fellow, taken from us far too soon."

Sam felt as if the bottom fell out of his belly. He collapsed back into the chair and stared at the far wall, as the barber continued.

"Are you sure?" Sam asked.

"I'm the barber, but I double as the undertaker. I ought to know if anyone does."

"Liam Stranahan, a little taller than me, black hair, brown eyes."

"I been cutting Liam's hair since he got to Phillipsburg. Did you know him?" he asked.

Sam didn't answer, then after a long moment, asked, "Who shot him?"

"Don't rightly know. Marshal's been investigating. Lots of folks heard the shot, but no one saw the scoundrel leave the livery . . . That's where it happened.

"There goes the marshal now, you want I should call him in?"

Sam glanced at the window, and saw a tall man ambling by. The man glanced in, but continued walking.

"No, no, if I need to see him, I'll drop by his office after you get me spiffed up."

The floor below the chair was covered in black hair when the barber handed Sam a small looking glass.

"What do you think?" he asked.

"It'll do, now the beard."

As the barber wrapped the hot towel around his face, Sam could hardly sit in the chair. His brother was dead. All this time, and he'd missed finding him by a week. If he'd been here a week ago, maybe . . . Sam's mind raced, but the only result was a hollow feeling in the pit of his gut. Then he realized it would stay with him until he found the man who'd killed his brother. He almost had to tear the towel away, as it blinded and seemed to suffocate him, but he contained his urge, and his rage. He had to shed the beard.

Who killed his brother? He had to know, and he had to avenge him. And he might as well begin right here. He controlled his tone. "So, who do you think killed Liam?"

"Well, there's a lot of talk about." As the barber answered, Sam could hear him stropping his razor again.

"And what's the talk?"

"First on the list would be his partner.

You know Gunter Kauffmann?"

"Never met the man. Partner in what?" He continued to interrogate the barber, talking through the towel, while his beard softened.

He learned about Miss Helen, the soiled dove, and all the details that were known about the day Liam had been gunned down. The barber went from stropping to the sound of the brush being worked to form up some lather for the job at hand.

Finally, Sam heard some movement in the room; then he felt the barber's hand on the towel, and the man began unwrapping it.

As quickly as he finished, the barber scrambled away.

Sam opened his eyes to see what the commotion was, and found himself staring into the business end of a double-barreled scattergun.

"I'm Marshal Clark Peckham, and you're Sam Stranahan, and you're under arrest for robbery and murder. I been expectin' you."

"I don't suppose the barber can finish this shave?" Sam asked.

"Nope. But you can unbuckle that belt, and just leave it lying in the chair. I'll come back and fetch it after I get you cozy in a cell."

"Can we talk about this? I got business I've got to take care of," Sam said, but with little enthusiasm, as he undid the belt and let it fall away.

"Soon as you're tucked away you can talk till hell freezes over. . . . That is unless you're hung first. Now, get up, and get movin'."

As they walked to the jail, Sam's curiosity got the better of him. "How did you recognize me?"

"The big blue stud."

"Wasn't on the poster."

"Judge Talbot wrote me a letter, and probably wrote all the other law officers in the country. Jud Peters was a friend of his. Would have been his son-in-law, had you not shot him down."

"And I suppose Judge Talbot will be the one doing the judging."

"That's the way it works, pardner. I didn't see your horse tied outside the barber's."

Sam eyed him a minute, then lied, "I sold him, to an old boy I met on the street. Needed a little money."

Gunter Kauffmann dismounted and

stomped up the stepping stones to Betsylou's. One of the girls was enjoying the warm winter sun by having her tea on the front porch.

"Where is dis Helen, or Maureen, or whatever her name is?"

"She's inside. I'll get her." The girl didn't like Gunter's attitude, and jumped up to run and find Maureen.

In a moment, Maureen appeared at the front door.

"I vant to buy yer interest in da mine," he stated, without any preliminaries.

"Not for sale, Mr. Kauffmann," she said and started to close the door.

He leaped forward and jammed a booted foot in the opening, then shoved the door open, knocking her back.

"There's a half dozen women here, Gunter. I wouldn't do anything foolish." Two of the girls were standing in the kitchen doorway, and another was sitting at one of the card tables.

"I vant to buy yer interest," he repeated.

"And I told you, I'm not interested in selling. I'm coming up there in a couple of days to take a look —"

"Da hell you are. I vill shoot anyone who comes on da property."

"Clark Peckham, will you shoot him? I'll

bring him along if need be."

He started to take another step forward, then heard the sound of hammers being racked back. He looked up to see the girl who had been on the front porch standing on the stairway, an old scattergun in hand, aimed at him.

"You vouldn't shoot me," he said, but his voice didn't sound convinced.

"I've shot a lot of birds on the wing, Mr. Kauffmann, and they were a lot smaller and a lot faster than you. You make a fine big target, Mr. Kauffmann."

He looked doubtful for only a moment, then reddened and spun on his heel and stomped out.

Maureen looked back over her shoulder. "Thank you, Sarah," she said in a low voice.

"I vill be back!" Kauffmann shouted as he mounted up, and whipped the horse into a gallop back down Broadway.

Silas waited until seven, when it was pitch-black outside. He had no money himself, and had left most all of his trading material back in old Hunting Hawk's camp.

So all he could do was stand in the fine saloon outside the restaurant, and watch the drinkers and see the patrons being served fat T-bone steaks, oysters, and other delights.

Finally, he walked outside and down Broadway, seeing if he could spot Sam.

It wasn't like the ol' coon not to do what he said he was going to do.

Hell, maybe he'd gone back to camp.

Silas set out at a stiff pace to find the ladies, and he hoped, Sam.

But when he arrived at their campfire, Sam had not returned.

Hell, had that little talk about Miss Mary scared him off? Silas doubted it.

So far, Sam hadn't seemed much scared of anything.

Miss Maureen O'Toole had no problem figuratively filling Betsylou's button shoes.

The place was packed with men, both card tables going strong, and the liquor and tokens flowing.

She looked across the room, and saw a man who was taller than most, and who had been a good customer of hers. But she was no longer taking customers upstairs, now that she was the madam of the house. Tom Beauchamp, one of the bartenders at the Kaiser, crossed the room with a big smile under his prominent nose. "Miss

Helen, or I guess it's Miss Maureen these days."

"That it is, Tom. How you been?"

"Fine, I see you're not occupied, how 'bout we go upstairs for a . . . for a little poke?" Tom was a bit of a bashful sort, and Maureen truly liked him. It was hard for her to say no to an old customer. But she did.

"Then how about me buying you a drink, Miss Maureen?"

"I thought you didn't drink, Tom."

"I don't, but I'll sure 'nuff buy you one."

"Let's go in the kitchen. I need a break. And I'll treat you to a cup of tea."

In moments they were seated at the kitchen table, a cup of hot tea in front of each of them.

"Do you think Liam's brother did this thing they're saying?" Tom asked.

"What about Liam's brother?"

"Peckham put him in the clinker a couple of hours ago."

"Liam's brother, here?"

"Yep, in the room with the iron walls."

"I've got to go," she said, jumping up. "Feel free to finish your tea."

She went into her private quarters, formerly Betsylou's private quarters, at the rear of the house and grabbed a wrap, and in moments was striding down the hill toward the marshal's office and jail.

Clark Peckham had hired a new deputy when Tucker Stark had become a resident of the jail, and Maureen hoped either he or Marshal Peckham would be in the office.

Terrence "Tuffy" Fordham, the new deputy, was sitting at Peckham's desk, eating a plate of food from Frenchy's. He was a round-faced blond young man, with a stringy stubble of a Vandyke beard and pork chop sideburns that barely colored his face. His round face was not out of place as he was round in the middle also, and at the moment, was doing what he could to increase his girth by stuffing his face with a heaping forkful of mashed potatoes and gravy. He stopped his fork midway when Maureen threw open the door, and he centered watery pale eyes on her. He dripped a little gravy on his already stained shirt, and cut his eyes down surveying the new spot as she spoke.

"I've got to see Mr. Stranahan," she said.

She'd never liked Fordham. He'd been a customer of the house for a while, until Miss Betsylou had told him not to bother to come around anymore. She'd caught him cheating at cards.

Fordham eyed her. "Well, Miss Helen —"

262

ns. "I'll be bringing Mr. Stranahan's
als to him, Deputy. So don't be feeding
any jail slop."

Maybe."

No maybe about it, Tuffy. I'll be here,
ne of the girls will, every mealtime.
derstand?"

it no rules against him being fed by
never." As she walked out the door,
him mumble, "Even a whore."

od a little taller, and walked with
lers thrown back.

cided she liked Sam Stranahan
d she was going to help him get
e, if there was any way she

ought there was a way.

"My name is Maureen, Maureen O'Toole,
and I'd like to see Mr. Stranahan."

"What's your business?"

She thought about that for a moment,
then said, "We're partners. Partners in the
Siglinda mine. We've got important things
to discuss."

He was disappointed that she seemed to
have a legitimate reason to visit with the
prisoner. Still, he hated to give in to her, he
figured he'd been treated badly at Betsylou's and had shed no tears when she'd
gone to meet her maker. He cleared his
throat. "I should ask Clark afore I let you
in there."

She thought about turning and leaving,
but she really wanted to see Liam's brother.
Instead, she walked over and perched on
the edge of the desk. "Look, Tuffy, does
Clark know you were a customer at
Betsylou's, and why she asked you to stay
away?" She stood and moved to the door
separating the cells from the office. "I bet
he'd think twice about your being a deputy,
if he knew you were a man no one would
play a game of cards with."

Fordham colored, and she could see the
muscles in his jaw working. He looked as if
he could spit nails, but instead, he stood and
walked around her and opened the door.

"Very kind of you, Deputy Fordham." She winked at him. "But that still doesn't mean you're welcome up on the hill." She slipped by him.

"If you got a pig sticker or a firearm hidden in that bustle, I'll see you hang as high as he does. I'll have to leave this door open," he said, then walked back to the desk.

There were no chairs in the hallway separating the cells. The two on her left were empty, the doors ajar. They were made of welded two-inch-wide flat bars, in a crisscross pattern with six-inch open squares between the horizontal and vertical quarter-inch-thick ribbons of iron. On the other side, the walls were solid sheet iron, riveted together. The iron door had several slits forming a window about head high, and a wider horizontal slit below, where she supposed food and whatnot could be passed through. She kept her back to the bars, and called out.

"Mr. Stranahan?"

Faces appeared at the openings in each of the two doors. The back cell housed a face she knew, Tucker Stark.

"You sure it's not me you came to visit, lil' lady?" Stark asked, but she ignored him.

"I'm Stranahan," the man behind the first door said.

"I'm Maureen O'Toole, Mr. and I was a . . . a friend of your

"I'd ask you to take a seat, M but I don't seem to have takin'."

"I'd as soon stand, thank

There was an awkward can I do for you?" Sam fin

"I guess the question is for you? You're the one se She giggled nervously.

"I just heard about m about Liam," he said pened."

They talked for Fordham checking or utes. Sam learned th the Siglinda, not o with the man su brother. And that the house that M overheard Kauffr one to shoot Maureen told F that man was cell. Finally, F doorway, and going, Miss soon."

As she l

264

Twenty

Late that night, after the lamp had gone out in the front office, Sam heard a light tapping on the metal wall separating the cells. A voice whispered, "You awake, friend?"

"I'm awake," Sam answered. There was a small crack in a joint of the metal, and Sam put his head closer.

"Tucker Stark, and you're Stranahan?"

"Yep."

"Relative of the ol' boy what got himself shot?"

"Brother."

"So, what brings y'all to the hospitality of Phillipsburg?"

"Wanted for robbery and murder, but I didn't do it." He could hear a low chuckle. "Nobody in these here places never did it."

"Suppose that's right," Sam said, and smiled tightly. "How about you?"

"Murder. . . . I shot up a bunch of card

cheats in a whorehouse, an' some folks got in the way."

"Pity. They gonna hang you?"

Again the chuckle. "I wouldn't be a damn bit surprised. It's probably time I made peace with the Maker. They gonna hang you?"

"It's not on my schedule, but then I guess it never is on the schedule of those who get their necks stretched."

They were silent for a long while; then Sam asked, "Did you know my brother, Liam Stranahan?"

"I knew of him. And I knew that low-life yellowbelly he was partnered up with."

"Kauffmann?"

"One and the same."

"Rumor was, he shot Liam?"

"No doubt about it. . . . Tol' me he did, from his very own lips."

"Why did he tell you?" Sam asked, suddenly very interested in what Stark had to say.

"For me to know. . . . I'm gonna get some shut-eye."

"Hold on, Stark. I was also told that Kauffmann hired you to shoot Liam down. Did you kill my brother?"

"You only got half the story, partner. Yeah, he tried to hire me . . . but your

268

brother didn't show up where he was supposed to. Next thing I know, Kauffmann is telling me he did the job hisself. I'm tellin' you on my old ma's grave, I done shot a lot of folks in my time, but your brother wasn't one of them. Hell, I don't even own no scattergun."

Sam said nothing more. He lay back and decided he, too, would try and get some sleep.

But it wouldn't be easy.

After a long while, the voice came through the crack again. "Hey, Stranahan. You think the good Lord really does forgive ever'thing, should a body come to him for such?"

Sam ignored him, and again tried to fall off to sleep.

When Silas came back into town with the rising sun and found the grulla still tied at the Kaiser hitching rail, it didn't take him long to find out that Sam was a guest of the territory in the Phillipsburg jail.

Silas went straight to the place and reached the front door the same time as did Marshal Clark Peckham. After the introductions, Silas asked, "I'd like to see Stranahan."

"He's not acceptin' calling cards at the

moment, Mr. McGraw. Come back after we've had our coffee, and we'll talk about why you got reason to see my prisoner."

"I can do that," Silas said, his tone accommodating, but when he walked out, he merely went around the building and found a cell window. It, too, was only slits in sheet iron, bolted to a brick wall.

"Sam," he called quietly.

"Silas."

He could hear Sam moving up close to the window.

"Sorry about the drink," the faceless voice said.

"Think nothin' of it. Place was a wee bit fancy for my taste, leastwise."

"I guess I shoulda stayed a bit shaggy. Come to think of it, I did get a free haircut out of the deal."

"Hell, son, you need to get this business straight with the law, so maybe now's as good a time as any."

"Afraid I can't do it in here, Silas. Hell, it's my word against the Bozeman sheriff, and as I told you, he was in cahoots on that robbery."

"And a lying lowlife Thacker is, too."

"Like I say."

"Then I guess we best be gettin' you outta there."

"Someone's coming. Silas, go see Miss Maureen O'Toole, at the brothel on the hill."

"Maureen . . ." he started to repeat, then heard a harsh voice from inside.

"Here's a basin and a little water so's you can wash up if'n you're a mind to. Set your chamber pot by the door, then back away and face the far wall. Legs and arms spread."

Silas slipped away.

After the sun was over the mountain, Miss Maureen showed up at the jail, a tray of food in hand.

Clark Peckham sat behind his desk. "Good morning," he offered.

"I got some breakfast for Mr. Stranahan," she said.

Tuffy Fordham sat on a low bench, under a rack of rifles and shotguns, on the far wall from Peckham. "I told her it was in the rules, Marshal," he said, but his voice rang hollow.

"Then come on in," Peckham said. "But set it down here on my desk, and let me check it."

She did as told, and Peckham picked up a fork and poked around in the scrambled eggs, fried potatoes, and the bowl of oatmeal. Then he set a biscuit off on his desk and eyed her. "I better check and make sure this ain't poison."

She flashed him her most coquettish smile. "Tomorrow, I'll bring some extra."

He walked to the connecting door and held it open for her.

When she approached Sam's cell, a voice rang out from the one next door. "Why, I don't suppose you'd be bringin' enough for me, lil' lady?"

Maureen set the tray in Sam's slot and waited for him to take it.

"Obliged, Miss Maureen," Sam said, but she didn't respond.

She did move to the cell next door, but stayed against the far wall, just out of his reach. "I might bring you a new rope to be hanged with, Tucker Stark, but that's all you'll be getting from any friend of Betsylou Maddigan."

He laughed. "She bit like a timber rattler, and got what she deserved . . . the no-account whore. I'll make do with beans and hardtack. Good jail fare."

She moved back to Sam's door, and chatted with him as he ate.

"Did Silas find you, Miss Maureen?"

"I've been over at Frenchy's, fetching your food."

"He'll be coming to see you. Silas McGraw, my very good friend."

"I'll look out for him," Maureen said, glancing up to see Peckham leaning on the doorjamb. "I'll pick up the breakfast dishes when I bring your lunch. You want something to read?"

"A *Leslie's*, or a local paper would be fine."

"I can do that," she said, and excused herself.

As she passed through the door, Peckham stood aside.

"Don't get too attached to Stranahan, Miss Maureen," Peckham said.

"And why's that, Marshal?"

"Judge Talbot will be in on the afternoon stage. He'll be tryin' Stark, and witnessing the hanging; then he and Fordham will be taking Stranahan back to Bozeman to be hanged."

"Don't you mean to be tried?"

Peckham merely laughed, and she walked away.

When she returned to the house, a grizzled old plainsman was sitting on her front porch, reclining in one of the wicker chairs, his moccasined feet up on the rail.

He dropped them to the porch and rose when she came through the gate.

"Ladies inside said you'd be back real soon," he said, pulling the old floppy-brimmed hat off his head.

"Silas Mc . . ."

"McGraw, young lady. Sam tolt me to come see you."

"So he told me," she said, walking past him and waving for him to follow.

"I'm going to buy you a cup of tea, Mr. McGraw, and you can tell me about Sam Stranahan."

"I'd favor coffee."

"And I like a straight-talkin' man. Coffee it is."

They visited for most of the morning.

Later in the afternoon, after lunch, and after boredom began to set in, Stark was again at the crack in the metal sheets.

"Stranahan?"

Yeah," Sam answered, moving closer to the crack.

"Who was it you done kilt?"

"Nobody, but the handbill is for a stage-coach robbery, just outside of Bozeman. Shotgun messenger name of Jud Pacovsky got himself shot by some highway-men, if you can call the sheriff and his gang highwaymen. Hell, I was down on the Yellowstone at the time, headin' for

Bozeman, not away."

"Norval and Gordy done it, them an' the old boy's brother. Actually it was the brother, a deputy sheriff, Rusty, I think it was, done shot him."

Again Sam was very interested in what Stark had to say. "You know these fellas, Norval and Gordy?"

"I know 'em, Hutchins and Pendergast. Not bad ol' boys, fair to middlin' shots, and good in the saddle. We was runnin' mates; how-some-ever, the som'bitches got real scarce when I got my tit in a crack up at that whorehouse. Come to think of it, I hope you do catch up with 'em, and plug 'em fulla holes."

"They were there . . . at Miss Maureen's place, I mean, right here in Phillipsburg?"

"Might *still* be right here in Phillipsburg, but don't be thinkin' they'll be standin' up for you at the risk of their own hides. They ain't that good fellows. Pendergast has a cousin or some such down Flint Creek a ways. He says the old boy has more'n a hundred hogs down in the Flint Creek bogs. If they ain't here, they're there."

"Hutchins and Pendergast . . . which is which?"

"Norval Hutchins and Gordy Pendergast, but they both got rewards out for them. Pendergast is worth seven hundred down in Salt Lake City, and Hutchins two hundred fifty over in Oregon. Hell, but none of this won't do you no good. They're halfway to Canada, if'n they got a brain."

"You're probably right, but it's good to know who you're hanging for."

Stark chuckled at that. "You could be a busy fella, what with that sauerkraut som'bitch on your list, and now Gordy and Norval."

"And me tucked up tight in a damned iron box."

Again, Stark chuckled. "You better be makin' yer own peace with the good Lord, Stranahan."

Late that afternoon, Silas McGraw entered the Phillipsburg Mercantile, the primary supplier of equipment for the local mining industry.

One of his many talents had been perfected as a deck hand on a Missouri riverboat. That was how he got to Montana Territory. He could handle lines with the best of them, and much of the cargo he'd moved had weighed many hundreds of pounds. He knew his lines, and how to make them work to best advantage.

He fished out two shiny ten-dollar gold pieces from his pocket, courtesy of a certain sportin' lady, and was pleased when he was only charged four dollars for a four-way block and tackle, and another two dollars for one hundred and fifty feet of three-quarter-inch hemp line, a dime for a bottle of coal oil, and a penny for a few sulfur heads.

For once he was mounted, riding Sam's grulla stud, but mounted on the animal astride a packsaddle with the bags rolled up and tied behind. When he exited the store, he unrolled and positioned the canvas bags before loading them with the block and tackle and the line, then having more than an adequate amount of change, proceeded to the Kaiser.

He'd left the ladies behind in camp, and felt a little guilty entering the Kaiser for some good whiskey and a pound of beefsteak, but not so guilty that he wouldn't do so. Besides, they were busy packing up. And again besides, they wouldn't be welcome there.

At six, Miss Maureen entered the marshal's office, carrying a tray. This time, Fordham was behind the marshal's desk. He poked through the bowl of stew on the tray, removed one of the big rolls, and eyed her as if she was going to complain, but she merely smiled and offered him some honey that was in a small bowl next to the rolls.

When she entered the jail, Sam was already at the door, having seen her coming through the small slotted window, where he could view about six feet of the street, if he strained.

"I saw Silas pass, riding my horse," he commented.

She passed the food through the slot, then waved him over. "Don't sleep too soundly. Silas is gonna come calling near to midnight."

"Pretty late for a visit," Sam said.

"Seemed like the best time to him," she said, and smiled. "I'll be waiting."

As he ate, she stayed and visited with him. Between bites, he asked, "Do you ever miss the old country?"

"I barely remember the place. I was a wee lass when I left there with my uncle and his sons. My ma and da thought it good to get me away, and we couldn't afford for all of us to come. I surely do miss my ma."

"Mine died here, in Missouri before I left home. A ma's a fine thing to have, and I surely miss mine also."

"Mine was a great one for poems and toasts and such. This one might suit you:

"May there always be work for your hands to do;

"May your purse always hold a coin or two;

"May the sun always shine on your windowpane;

"May a rainbow be certain to follow each rain;

"May the hand of a friend always be near you;

"May God fill your heart with gladness to cheer you."

"Aye," Sam said, "I'm hoping there'll be a rainbow following this squall." It was all he could get out, his throat suddenly going thick. The rhyme made him think of his brother, who'd been a great one for toasts. He hoped, as his brother often said of those departed, that Liam had reached heaven at least an hour before the devil knew he was dead.

As they talked, three blocks away Silas was ordering dinner, seated at a table with a white cloth, from a waiter in a clean white shirt.

There was a good chance it might be his last good meal for a few years should his plan be thwarted by the law, and that fact assuaged his guilt.

By nine o'clock that night, he was well fed and a little tipsy, but not so much that he couldn't take care of business.

Again leaving the grulla tied at the Kaiser, he set out up the hill on foot, carrying only the bottle of coal oil and the matches in his pocket. He ducked behind the buildings, avoiding being seen. Earlier in the day, he'd made the same trip on horseback, and knew exactly where he was heading. About a half mile out of town, on the road to Granite, sat an old log warehouse. It hadn't been occupied since the boom in the sixties, and Silas figured it wouldn't be much of a loss.

When he reached there, he knew he was early, so he took his time. On the hillside that toed out just at the rear of the log structure, he gathered whatever trash he could find, and piled it against the back of the log wall. It had taken him fifteen minutes to reach the place, another half hour spent gathering trash, and would take him another fifteen minutes to get back to the grulla, and another to get set up.

Hell, he still had the better part of an hour to waste. He lay down out of sight of the road and watched the stars, until he was sure he had spent an hour waiting.

Then he went to the trash pile, sprinkled it with some coal oil, and doused the logs above it with more, then lit up. Quicker than he would have believed, the building was aflame.

Twenty-one

Silas ran down the road for a quarter mile, then cut off and went cross-country until he was behind the row of buildings fronting the main street. By the time he made his way between the buildings and found himself on Broadway, the fire bell was clanging and men were running toward the firehouse.

He moved quickly and fetched the grulla. As he did so, a four-up was hitched and the fire wagon rolled out of the firehouse. Those not riding were running up the hill. As Silas led the grulla down Broadway, Fordham, the deputy, ran past, following the others up the hill.

Silas passed the marshal's office, and could see no one at the desk inside. As he had hoped, everyone had responded to the fire, either to help or merely to watch the show.

Passing the next two buildings, Silas finally cut between two and made his way back to the alley, then back up it to the rear of the jail. There were only three or four paces between the jail and the building next door, and he didn't have much room to work. He had noted a one-foot-diameter ponderosa pine growing up tight against the building next door, and it would do. He threw a couple of loops through the slots of the iron plate bolted to the brick wall, and immediately received the silent help of Sam inside. Then he went to the pine, and double-looped it. When both were set, he rigged the hooks of the block and tackle up to each set of loops, and the end of its line to a makeshift double-loop collar around the grulla's neck.

By the time he had the block and tackle rigged, he was hearing noise from the cell next to Sam's.

"What's going on out there? Hey, you. Y'all don't get me outta here too, I'm gonna yell out."

Sam took the time to move to the other cell window. "You yell out, and I'll empty this old Colt of mine through that window. I'd keep my trap shut, were'n I you."

The voice silenced.

"Stand aside," Silas whispered through Sam's window; then he moved to the grulla and took up his reins. He moved the big horse back toward the alley, taking up the slack. The animal leaned into the work, but nothing happened, other than a low grating sound. Had he been able to pull directly perpendicular to the wall, it would have been no problem, but pulling at a sharp angle made the job much tougher.

"Give it a jerk," Sam advised from inside.

Silas backed the horse a half dozen feet, then smacked him a good one on the rear, the animal charged into the traces, and this time the wall groaned loudly.

"Don't break the damned line," Sam advised, through the slits.

"Shut up, youngster," Silas said. "I was doin' this kinda work when you was a glimmer in some Irish lout's eye," and backed the horse again.

This time he not only smacked, but gave a rebel yell. The iron window did not break away from the wall, but rather, the whole wall gave way, leaving a ragged four-by-four-foot hole that Sam scrambled through, coughing because of the dust raised.

Sam clambored across the rubble and flashed Silas a smile.

They cast the block and tackle and

makeshift collar off the animal, and both mounted. In a heartbeat, the big grulla was pounding down the alley at a full gallop, with Tucker Stark screaming behind them.

"Ungrateful som'bitch," he yelled, over and over.

When they reached camp, the ladies were seated at the campfire, but all the stock was packed.

"Did you get some of my money for the rigging?" Sam asked Silas as the ladies mounted up.

"Nope, didn't want to waste time coming back to camp. Miss Maureen was more than happy to fork up two ten-dollar gold pieces. Seems she had a hankerin' for your brother."

"Where are you and the ladies off to, Silas?"

"They's a nice little pass to the west of here, and the headwaters of a fine creek, Rock Creek they call it, that works its way down a long valley to the Clark Fork. I favor it to winter up. It's a mite heavy in snow, but they's plenty of critters about, and I got the start of a good cabin there." Then he realized what Sam had asked. "You mean you're not agoin' with us, ol' coon?"

"I'm going for a couple of miles; then I'm cuttin' back. I got a debt to repay with Miss Maureen, and another kind of debt with a fella named Gunter Kauffmann . . . and a mess to straighten up with the law."

"Well, ol' coon, we could just keep a-movin' west."

"And keep watchin' for handbills. No, thanks, Silas."

"I'll be goin' along with you. . . ."

"No, you won't. You'll take care of Talking Woman and Miss Mary, and I'll take care of this. You keep lookin' into the morning sun, and I'll be along in a week or so, God willin' and the creek don't rise. You've done far too much already, old friend." Sam had unrolled his buffalo robe and draped it over his shoulders, and he dug his little possibles bag out of his saddlebags and fished out five twenty-dollar gold pieces. He handed them to Silas. "This'll keep you and the ladies till I get back."

"Don't need no cash where I'm a-goin'," Silas said, trying to refuse the money.

"Then don't use it, if you don't need it. If you do, I'd feel real bad if you didn't have it."

"Fair enough," Silas said, taking the coins.

It was a quarter hour before Sam reined away, without saying another word.

The McGraws reined up in the darkness and watched him for a moment until he was out of sight, wondering if they'd ever see him again.

After the excitement of the fire died out, as did the fire, both Clark Peckham and Tuffy Fordham returned to the jail. They found the gaping hole, and Tucker Stark banging away on the wall not far from the hole, trying to make his own. But his effort was to no avail.

"Nothin' we can do tonight," Peckham said, his jaw gnawing in anger. "In the morning, we'll find out if anyone knows where that block and tackle came from, but right now I want to have a little talk with one of Mr. Sam Stranahan's admirers up on the hill. Who knows? Maybe the old boy found himself a room and warm bed up there."

"She did it," Tuffy said, "sure as whores is goin' to hell's fires, she did it."

"I can't see Miss Maureen rigging a block and tackle, but she sure coulda put some damn fool up to it."

Clark Peckham mounted the skunk-striped dun he rode, and put the reins to the animal, loping up Broadway and to the edge of town, then slid to a stop in front of Miss Maureen's Sporting House, the place's new name.

He tied the dun and stomped across the yard and up the stairs. The place was full of customers, drinkers, and cardplayers. He spied Miss Maureen at the bar, talking with a couple of well-dressed townspeople, and walked over and took her by the upper arm, almost dragging her back outside.

"What the —" she complained.

As he closed the door behind them, she snapped, "What the hell do you think you're doing, Clark Peckham?"

"We're gonna have a talk," he said, poking a finger at her breastbone.

"That's fine. But we're not gonna have a talk out here. It's cold. Let's go in my kitchen, and you can have a drink."

"I'm not drinkin' your whiskey."

"I meant a cup of tea or coffee, but you can have whiskey if you prefer."

She led the way back through the sitting room and dining room, which was now silent as the men watched the small procession.

When the kitchen door closed behind them, she snapped, "Now, Marshal, just what's so important that you have to stomp around in my place of business, acting like the cock of the walk?"

"Stranahan. He broke out of my jail. . . . In fact, he destroyed the damn place."

She had to turn away to keep from smiling, and did so in order to brew two cups of tea. When she turned back, she could see he was still fuming. "Now, Clark, what would I know about that? Pshaw, Marshal, I was hopin' you'd hang him. One less partner to worry about."

That shocked Peckham, and he was silent, as he raised the cup to his mouth, then winced. "Damn, that's hot, woman."

"So, when did all this happen?"

"Earlier tonight. Somebody hitched a block and tackle up to a team of horses, and jerked the whole damn jail wall down."

She suddenly looked sincerely concerned. "Did Tucker Stark escape?"

"No, he was trying to when we got there, but we moved him to the other side. Somebody started that fire up the hill, so as to cover their corruption."

"I can't imagine."

"I can. You sure you didn't have nothin' to do with this, Maureen?"

"Let me see, I used to use a block and tackle when I was a freighter, out in the Judith Basin, then when I was a hardrock miner, down at Bannack. These fancy bustles sure did get in the way, how-some-ever. . . ." She couldn't help but laugh as he was beginning to redden.

"This is not humorous, Maureen. All right, you couldn't have done it yourself, but you could have hired —"

"Hired someone to break my partner out of jail? A wanted killer? I'm going to break him out so he can split up the take from the Siglinda, and maybe murder me if he doesn't like the way I bat my eyes at him?

"I was only nice to him so I could buy out his interest, before Kauffmann had a chance to get it. As you yourself said, I got one partner you and I both suspect of being a killer, and one you had in jail for murder. You don't really think . . ."

Peckham shook his head. "I guess this was a fool's errand." He sighed deeply. "If the offer still stands, I'll have that whiskey."

She sighed every bit as deeply as he had, as she went to fetch his drink.

Sam staked the grulla out in the brush near the edge of town, but out of sight of passersby. Then he headed for the livery, the Winchester in hand. It was no problem jimmying the simple lock, and he entered and climbed into the hayloft. He could still catch a few hours' sleep before the sun rose.

Erik Vandermer was an early riser, and arrived just as the sun was casting an orange light across the valley.

He unknowingly accommodated Sam by climbing up into the hayloft in order to fork hay down to his tenants. His eyes widened when Sam stepped out of the darkness of a corner, and had the Winchester leveled at the big man.

"What the —"

"I'm not here to harm you, Mr. Vandermer, or to rob you. I just want a little information. I'm Sam Stranahan, and my brother was shot dead here in your place."

"That's true. What can I tell you?"

"What happened?"

"I don't truly know." He walked to the edge of the loft and pointed down. "Your brother was found there, about ten feet from the front doors."

"I presume being hit with a shotgun blast in the chest would have knocked him back a ways."

"The marshal and I figured he was standing about there." He pointed a few feet closer to the rear doors. "And the shooter was over there, about fifteen feet from Liam."

"And did Liam have a weapon?"

"He did, a side arm. And it was drawn and one shot had been fired."

"My brother was a fair shot, and a calm and collected sort. Did he hit this shooter?"

"I didn't think so until a couple of days later, when I was mucking out down below. I did find some blood sign back near where I thought this damned assassin was standing."

"So you think the man was hit? Any idea where?"

"I have no way of knowing that."

"I thank you for your time, and hope I didn't take any years off your life, aiming this thing at you. You stay put up here in the loft for about ten minutes, and you'll come to no harm."

Vandermer merely nodded.

Sam went to the ladder and worked his way down, then out the back doors and back across a field to Blue, mounted, and headed out into the brush and circled around until he could again tie the horse out of sight. He had one more call to make before he could ride out of Phillipsburg.

Twenty-two

Judge Horace Talbot had come in on the afternoon stage, and gone straight to bed in the best room the Kaiser had to offer. He had no idea about the excitement that took place while he slept, until he limped down to breakfast. He'd sent a message the afternoon before for Marshal Clark Peckham to meet him in the restaurant, and Peckham was waiting when the judge arrived.

"Clark, I hear you had a little excitement at the jail last night. I trust my defendant is still with us?"

"Yes, sir. And when do you want to get at it?"

"I'll interview him this morning, and select a jury this afternoon. I'd suggest you start rounding up your witnesses and have them at the Miner's Hall. . . . I presume that's still where we'll be having our trial . . . by nine o'clock in the morning."

"Should I start having a gallows built?"

"If things were as you said in your letter, I'd say that would be fitting. I'd sure like to be taking Stranahan back to Bozeman when we're through here."

"I've put the word out, Judge."

"How about a posse?"

"No trail to follow, and nobody saw them ride out of town. We'll get him, unless he hightails it out of the territory."

"Get him before I leave town, Clark. I hate to go home empty-handed."

"We'll get him."

Sam had ridden way around the north side of town, but noticed the cemetery down below where he sat the grulla. He couldn't help himself, and reined down and dismounted. It wasn't hard to find Liam's plot. There were three fresh graves. One belonging to Hardy McGregor was next to Liam's. William Smithson, the banker, was nearby, but in a fenced-in plot with room for a half dozen more graves. Sam knew there were two more recent burials, and presumed they were off away somewhere in the county plots.

Sam stood with hat in hand, staring down at the simple wooden marker. He calculated Liam's age, and realized he was only thirty-two, only two years older than he was himself. Too damned young to be under six feet of soil.

He vowed again that he would avenge his brother, then turned and worked his way out of the cemetery and back to the grulla.

It was a fairly tough ride up to the Siglinda mine, but he found it easily, following Maureen's instructions.

When he could see the mine up ahead, with its few tailings and single cabin, he dismounted and led Blue off into the pines and tied the big horse, then slipped the Winchester from its sheath and worked his way along the slope opposite the mine opening. Tendrils of smoke wove themselves into one as they climbed from the chimney. There was one added feature that Maureen hadn't mentioned. A walled tent sat a little closer to the stream than did the cabin. It too had a chimney, and it too was smoking.

Sam found a good spot under a ponderosa where he could see both cabin and mine mouth, and sat down to wait and observe.

A big man that Sam presumed was Kauffmann appeared in the mine opening, and yelled impatiently down at the tent. "Woo, where the hell are you?"

In a moment, a Chinaman appeared at

the tent flap, carrying a coal-oil miner's lamp, and hurried up to the mine and disappeared inside.

For the next hour, this man, Woo, and another Chinese appeared at the mine opening intermittently to dump tailings from baskets into the growing pile descending from the mine opening to the valley floor forty feet below.

When the sun was high in the sky, both Chinese appeared, dumped their baskets full of debris, and then headed down the hill to their tent.

In moments, the big man came out and clambored down the hill to the cabin. The fire had died as had the smoke in both chimneys, but soon both were roiling out smoke.

Dinnertime, Sam thought. *Hell, I could use some chow.*

He worked his way around, crossing the stream, then along the other mountain face until he came even with the cabin. Dropping down alongside the timber walls, he inched forward until he rounded the front corner and was face-to-face with the door. The tent flap on the wall tent was down, so he wouldn't be seen by the Chinese unless they came out to head back up to the mine, but he figured they'd take at least a half hour, and it hadn't been more than fifteen minutes.

He tested the lever on the door and it moved freely, so he shoved, and the door swung back.

Gunter sat on a cot, a bowl balanced on his knees, a surprised look on his face.

"You got enough for two, Kauffmann?" Sam said, and strode in, the Winchester hanging loosely at his side.

"Who the hell are you? That whore send you here?" He set the bowl on the cot and started to rise.

Sam brought the Winchester up and waved him back down. Kauffmann hesitated a minute, and Sam said, "Sit. Now."

He returned to his spot on the cot, and calmly picked his bowl back up and took a spoonful of whatever it was he had.

"There is more in the pot," he said with no emotion.

Sam made no move toward the stove. "Liam Stranahan sent me here, Kauffmann. He wants someone to get even for him being shot down like a dog."

"Then what you doing here? You should be somewhere where Liam's killer is."

"You're that man, Kauffmann."

"The hell you say," Kauffmann said, not

taking his eyes off the bowl, continuing to eat.

"Set the bowl down and take off your shirt."

Kauffmann eyed him calmly. "My men will come running if I call, and there vill be three guns to yer one."

"No, there will be two to my one, because I'll shoot you full of holes the minute you yell out. Now, take the shirt off, then your trousers if need be."

Kauffmann rose, and walked over to the stove and set the bowl down next to the pot. He pulled the shirt away and flung it into a corner, but had on a red union suit underneath.

"The trousers, then the long johns," Sam said.

Turning his back to Sam as if he was modest, Gunter grabbed the pot handle, spun, and flung the hot mixture of soup at Sam.

Sam ducked to the side and avoided the boiling mixture, but Kauffmann was on him before he could recover, knocking the Winchester out of his hands, and flailing at him with his fists. He slammed two hard blows to the sides of Sam's head before Sam could regain his footing, knocking him back against the cabin wall.

The blows had Sam reeling, but his backbone flooded with heat. This was the man who'd killed Liam. This was the man who'd kept him from ever seeing his brother again.

Sam exploded off the wall, first kicking the man coming at him, sinking a booted toe deep into his ample gut; then he smashed two hard blows to the German's face, and blood splattered from his nose.

The big man reeled back, then dove for Sam's Winchester and had it in hand, but before he could turn, Sam was on his back and also had the rifle gripped in both hands, straddling the man from behind. He jerked the weapon back, harder, harder, driving it into Kauffmann's throat, the steel barrel a garrote. He got a knee in Kauffmann's back, and with all his strength pulled the weapon back, cutting off the big man's wind.

Kauffmann was a strong man, but he could get no leverage against the rifle. Finally, he slumped, and his grip on the weapon lessened. Sam dropped a hand from the barrel end, and smashed Kauffmann again and again into the side of his head.

Kauffmann spun away, but was greatly weakened and Sam was able to jerk the rifle free of his grip. Both of Kauffmann's hands went to his throat as he tried desperately to regain his wind, but it wasn't soon enough.

Sam swung the rifle butt hard, catching Kauffmann alongside the skull. He went down in a heap. As a precaution, Sam slammed another booted toe deep into his gut. Kauffmann merely grunted, out cold.

Sam let his eyes sweep the small cabin until they centered on a five-gallon keg. Just as he started for it, a loud rap sounded through the door, which had been knocked closed in the scuffle.

Sam moved to the door and flung it aside with one hand, and shoved the Winchester through the opening with the other. The two Chinese stood there, startled. They scrambled back a few steps.

"You understand me?" Sam asked, and both nodded. "Then you go back to your business. I'm an owner in this mine, and I'll see you get paid. Don't worry about what's happening here, just a little disagreement between partners." They looked skeptical, but turned away and went back to their wall tent.

Sam went to the keg and slopped out a large dipperful of water, then flung it in Kauffmann's face.

It took another before the man sputtered and came to.

He started to rise, but Sam stopped him. "Don't get up, Kauffmann. Peel the trousers off and the long johns, right there, flat on the deck."

Kauffmann eyed him, utter hate glowing in his eyes, but he did as instructed, having to remove his brogans first. Finally, he got to the union suit. The wound in his side was still puckered and red, but was healing nicely.

"Too bad Liam was off by about three inches, or I wouldn't have had to make this trip up here."

"I fell, in the mine. Stuck a pick in my side."

"I'll stick one in your rotten heart if you don't get dressed. You're taking a walk down the mountain."

"I got a horse."

"Horse is too good for you. Now get dressed."

In fifteen minutes, Gunter Kauffmann, with a loop around his neck, was leading Sam and the grulla back down the mountain trail toward Phillipsburg.

I got him, now what the hell am I going to do with him? Sam thought, as he plodded along behind the big German.

But when they neared town, he had an idea. Maureen had told him how much she hated Kauffmann, so maybe she would help out. When he neared the hill with Maureen's house sitting atop it, he dismounted and led Kauffmann off into the woods and tied him securely to a tree. He mounted and galloped to the rear of Maureen's house, slipped in the back door, and moved through her quarters. He found her in the kitchen, making an afternoon snack for the ladies.

"I need your help," he said, ignoring one of the girls sitting at the kitchen table, sipping tea.

"What can I do?" she asked.

He waved her back into her quarters. "I've got Kauffmann tied up out in the woods. You got a cellar?"

"A potato cellar. It's not much."

"He doesn't rate much. I'm going to try and find two more owl hoots who owe me. Have you found out if Pendergast and Hutchins are here in town?"

"They headed out of town just after Stark shot up the place. Rumor is they're down the creek at some cousin's hog farm."

"How do I find it?" Sam asked.

Maureen smiled. "I'm told you can smell

it long before you can see it. It's right off the creek. You can't miss it."

"Then I'm off. When I handle this chore, then I'm gonna go find the man that can straighten this all out."

"If you mean Judge Talbot, he's here in town. I got a notice from the marshal today that I was to be at Miner's Hall at nine in the morning to serve as a witness in Stark's trial."

"I'm not telling you that I'm going to face some judge, even if I might be. What you don't know, you can't get in trouble for. And remember, you don't know that Gunter Kauffmann is tied up not ten feet beneath your house. Where's the root cellar?"

"You get into it on that side of the house." She pointed the way.

"I'm taking him down there, and tying him and blindfolding him. You can check up on him once in a while to make sure he stays well bound, but don't say anything and he won't know who it is . . . just in case this all doesn't go as I've planned."

"I'll keep the girls in the kitchen for an hour, to make sure none of them see you."

He headed for her back door.

"Sam," she called out and he turned back. "Be careful."

He smiled, and left.

As the big grulla loped down Flint Creek, Sam remembered why he didn't have to be quite so careful about how he treated Pendergast and Hutchins. . . . Both of them were wanted men, if Stark knew what he was talking about. Not that he wouldn't have shot Kauffmann down if he had had to.

As he moved along the beautiful flat valley floor, with the winding oxbow creek to his right, the cloud cover began to darken. By the time he'd ridden five miles, it began to blow, and to snow. Dark was only about an hour away, and it would be hard going with his face into the wind. The Flint Creek Valley had narrowed, and he was forced up on the side hill from time to time, his lope reduced to a steady but fast walk.

He worried he'd miss the ranch, but as promised, and with the wind in his face, he smelled it long before he saw the light of a cabin window.

Again, he tied the grulla up the hill in a pine copse, and worked his way back to the ranch. Even had the moon been out, it would have been dead dark. The cloud cover was thick, and it was still snowing.

As he neared, he realized there were two buildings and a privy. One was a small barn of probably six or eight stalls. Beyond the buildings were a number of small pens, which Sam presumed were birthing pens for the hogs. He knew enough about hogs to know you had to keep the sows apart from the herd when they were about to drop their litters.

Some of the pens seemed to be full of shoats, and some of sows with litters.

All of them were making plenty of noise.

He made his way to the barn and found six stalls, five of them occupied with a single horse each.

I wonder if there are five men here, Sam worried. But he had no choice, these two could clear him, and he was going to get his name right with the law.

Twenty-three

The last stall in the pig farm's barn was unoccupied, but then Sam looked again.

Two bedrolls were laid out on a bed of hay on the floor of the stall. Made sense, he thought, as the cabin seemed no more than a single room, and five bedding down would have been crowding things, if five stabled horses meant five riders.

If that was the case, it meant two of them would be coming back to the barn when it was bedtime.

He had no desire to try and take on five men, so he decided to wait in the cold and darkness, and hope against hope that these two beds belonged to Pendergast and Hutchins, and not to a couple of hired hands.

As he nuzzled down into the snow, he wished he had brought his buffalo robe, but it was tied behind the grulla's saddle back up in the pines. So he covered up with one of the bedrolls, and waited.

He snapped awake as his chin hit his chest. Having no way to judge the time, he hoped he hadn't actually been asleep. He was tempted to get up and go and try to listen at the window, as it seemed like it must be at least midnight.

Even with the bedroll as a cover, he was cold to the marrow.

Finally, he heard voices, and the barn door creaked as it opened, and the light of a lantern danced through the barn.

"You som'bitch, you won too damn many hands. You had to be cheatin'."

"Never cheat," the other said.

Sam could tell by the voices that they were drunk. Maybe it was a good thing that they had taken their time, and he guessed, played a little poker or something.

"The hell you don't. I seen you cheat sometimes."

"That was other folks, Norval. I mean I never cheat my friends."

"You ain't never had a friend, you som'bitch."

But the other man merely laughed. At least Sam was sure he had Norval Hutchins about to look down the barrel of his Winchester. Now if the other one was Pendergast . . .

The stall gate was pulled aside, and light flooded the stall where Sam crouched, rifle in hand.

"Don't move," Sam said, but Norval Hutchins reacted immediately, slapping for his side arm, as Pendergast threw the lantern at Sam.

Sam's rifle roared, and Hutchins was blown back across the barn. Pendergast broke for the barn doors, and with the lantern now in the stall, Sam could barely see his target. He dropped to one knee outside the stall, and fired low. It would do him little good to have two dead men on his hands. He needed them alive.

The running man spun and hit the ground, grasping at his leg with one hand, and at his side arm with the other.

"Don't pull that, or you're a dead man."

"You shot me, fool. You shot me. I'm gonna lose my leg. Damn you. Damn you," he cried, but he didn't pull the weapon.

"Now two-finger it out and throw it in that stall."

As he spoke, he approached the man slowly. Hutchins was on the ground behind them, but he was moaning quietly.

Just as Sam reached the man he presumed was Pendergast, a shot of light from the door of the cabin made him raise his eyes away from the man on the ground. A body filled the cabin doorway, and Sam snapped off a shot from the hip, not wanting to hit the man, only wanting to drive him back into the cabin. The shot worked, and the door slammed behind him.

The man on the ground was eyeing him as he pulled the revolver out of its holster with two fingers, as if he had something in his mind.

"I'd as soon blow a hole in you as look at you, Pendergast."

"How'd you know my name?"

"I didn't, but I do now. You're Gordon Pendergast, and you're going back to Phillipsburg with me and your friend back there."

"The hell you say. Horsebackin' would kill me with this leg all shot up."

"Then you're gonna die."

"Who are you?"

"I'm the man wanted for what you did in Bozeman, and you're gonna set it right with the law."

"Stranahan?"

"One and the same. Stay in the doorway where I can see you." Sam walked back and found the lantern and turned it up, just as what he thought was a death rattle came from where Hutchins lay. He took a look at Norval Hutchins as he returned, but the man was now not making a move or sound, and the ground under him was covered with foamy lung blood.

He moved back to the barn door and set the lantern a few feet from Pendergast. "Stay there and don't move."

"I need to get something around this thigh, afore I bleed out."

"Take your belt off and use it. How many are in the cabin?"

"Just one ol' boy, cousin Ezra Hutchins, his woman and daughter."

"Don't move." Sam slipped away to the cabin, now darkened as the light had been extinguished. He kept his back to the wall and sidled up to the window. "Hello, the cabin."

"What the hell do you want? I got women in here, so don't be shootin'."

I'm taking your kin back to Phillipsburg. You can stay holed up in there . . . and live. Or you can stick your head out again and get it shot off."

"Hell's fire, I ain't got no problem with you takin' 'em off. They eat like beggars and don't do no work."

"Then stay holed up until we get out of here."

"I'm going to bed with my woman."

"Good idea."

Sam returned to the barn and saddled the two horses that Pendergast said were theirs; then he hauled Hutchins up, draped him over the saddle, and tied the body in place. To an abundance of moans and groans, he got Pendergast in the saddle, bound his hands to the horn, and tied his ankles from one to the other with a rope under the horse's belly.

It wouldn't be a pleasant ride, as it was still snowing, but Sam felt like whistling. With any luck at all, he was about to resolve his problems with the law, and he was about to revenge Liam. He was far warmer on the return trip, wrapped in the buffalo pelt, thanks to Silas McGraw, than was either Pendergast or Hutchins. Then again, Hutchins couldn't have cared less, and Pendergast's complaining kept Sam awake and entertained.

It was near dawn when they limped up to Miss Maureen's Sporting House.

Sam rode right up to the hitching rail and tied Blue, then Pendergast's horse. Hutchins's horse was tied to Pendergast's.

Miss Maureen met him at the front door with two cups of coffee in hand. "I'm glad to see you. I was worried." She looked

311

more than merely worried as she handed him a cup.

"Hutchins is dead," he offered, "but Pendergast only has a little hole in his thigh. Don't think it got the bone, but he thinks he's about dead. Is Kauffmann still where I left him?"

"No, Sam, he got away."

"Damn. Any idea where?"

"He went straight down to Clark Peckham's office, or so Peckham told me when he showed up here last night, huntin' you."

"How did he get away?"

"One of the girls found him. She was down there looking for some onions, and cut him loose. I'm sorry, I had no idea. The girls never go down there. You said to act like I didn't know he was there, so I didn't warn them."

"Not your fault. I'm just glad he didn't come in here giving you grief . . . or worse."

"What are you going to do?"

"Well, it's pretty damn sure he didn't try to ride back to the mine last night. You think he'll be at the Kaiser?"

"It's a good bet."

"I've got to go there anyway, so I might as well take care of him one more time. It sure as hell isn't over, until he pays for Liam."

"Again, Sam, be careful."

"I hate to ask you, but could you watch Pendergast while I see if I can collect Kauffmann again? Then I've got to have a little talk with the judge."

"Whatever I can do . . ."

"You might see what you can learn about his role in the Bozeman robbery."

"I'll do that."

"Tell the old boy you won't do anything for his leg, or give him food or water until he fesses up. He seems real proud of that leg and doesn't want to lose it. Get some of the girls to help you get him inside, or down to the cellar. Keep his hands tied, and he'll be little trouble. He's both cold *and* yellow to the bone."

Maureen smiled. "I can imagine that he wants to keep his leg. I'll toughen up, Sam, and get what I can out of him. Maybe if I get the kitchen knives out and tell him we're gonna saw that leg off if he doesn't speak up . . ."

Sam smiled and nodded, then left.

As he was walking out to Blue, he heard Miss Maureen call out, "Sam, be careful, Kauffmann's a mean, rotten son of a bitch, and he'll be watching for you this time."

Sam waved over his shoulder, and mounted Blue.

"You ain't leavin' me here," Pendergast yelled after him as he rode away.

"The ladies said they'd be happy to saw that leg off for you, should you give them any trouble. You'll be fine . . . if you get rid of that wound and they get you a peg or a good crutch."

"What! What the hell are you talking . . ."

His voice faded as Sam gave his heels to Blue, and the big horse took up a lope down to the Kaiser.

Sam arrived at the rear of the hotel and tied the grulla, then walked around to the front. The desk clerk was just returning from the kitchen, with a cup of coffee in hand, when Sam boldly sauntered up to the desk.

"Howdy," Sam said. "Kauffmann down to breakfast yet?"

"Do you see him in there, friend?"

The man's manner was a bit on the haughty side, as he looked Sam up and down. Sam realized he was probably due the dubious look, as he'd been riding for miles in the weather, and had Pendergast's blood on his sleeve.

Sam managed to give the man a foolish grin. "Been riding all night to get here to my meeting with Kauffmann. I got a list of mining equipment for sale up in Butte, and we got to get at it afore the auction up there starts."

"I'm sure he'll be down soon."

So he was here in the Kaiser. "Maybe I'd better go up and get started while he cleans up."

"He don't have no ditty bag with him." The man continued to eye him suspiciously.

"Well, he wants this list. What room's he in?"

"Seven, at the rear, but you should wait."

"Thanks, friend," Sam said. He'd left the Winchester just outside the front door, and went to fetch it. When he returned with it in hand, the clerk gave him an even more dubious stare. When he headed for the stairway, the man's voice rang out.

"You can't go up there if you ain't a guest."

Sam didn't bother to give him a look, but took the stairs two at a time.

He strode straight to the rear of the hotel, and kicked the door to number 7 so hard it knocked the bottom hinge loose.

The door hung open, and Sam charged in.

Kauffmann stood at a white china bowl with a towel in both hands, wiping his face dry.

"What the —"

Sam crossed the room as Kauffmann dove for his side arm, hanging in its belt and holster from a hook on the wall. But Sam was too fast, and drove the butt of the Winchester into Kauffmann's belly as he reached for his weapon, doubling him over. He came up charging Sam, slamming into him and driving him back, knocking the Winchester to the floor. Both of them crashed through the window and out onto the second-story outside walkway.

They both regained their feet and began raining blows upon each other.

Judge Horace Talbot arose early, and took his time getting ready for the day. The witnesses had all been notified, the jury selected, and the hall was set up and ready. He was dressed and would have an early breakfast, which he hoped he'd somewhat wear off before he had to pick up the gavel. Of late, he'd been getting sleepy on the bench and at one time had even nodded off during testimony. He didn't want that to happen again.

As he was about to leave his room, he heard a crashing and banging outside his room, on the walkway that ran alongside the hotel. His room was one of only two that opened to both the inside hall and the outside walkway.

He turned and moved back to the outside door to see what the commotion was all about.

When he opened the door, a bloodied man lit flat on his back just outside, and then another fell on him and drove two hard blows to his face. His eyes rolled up in his head, and he didn't move. The man on top got to his feet as the judge backed away, wondering why he'd been so foolish as to open the door.

"Who are you?" the man snapped at him.

The judge puffed up his chest, and glowered at the ruffian. "I'm Federal Judge Horace Talbot, young man."

"Just the fellow I want to see," Sam said, and stepped inside the judge's door.

Twenty-four

Judge Horace Talbot eyed Sam with apprehension. "Looks to me like you have business with the marshal, not with me."

"No, sir," Sam said, and reached down and dragged Kauffmann in behind him. "This fellow here shot my brother, Liam Stranahan, and I've got proof he did."

"You're Stranahan, Sam Stranahan?" the judge asked, backing toward the door.

"You're not leaving, Judge, until you hear me out."

"You shot down my future son-in-law, and I got nothing to say to you."

"Rusty Pacovsky shot Jud Pacovsky, while he was robbing the stage in league with his partner, Sheriff Hiram Thacker. He was accompanied by Norval Hutchins, who I put a bullet in last night, down Flint Creek a ways, and by Gordon Pendergast, who I'm holding up the hill a ways."

A puzzled look crossed Talbot's face.

"You're saying Hiram Thacker is a thief? That's hard to believe."

"Rusty Pacovsky confessed that very thing to me, after I put a bullet in him up on Deep Creek."

"I saw that Rusty was shot up, but he was after you as a legal deputy."

"He confessed to me in front of Silas McGraw. And your prisoner, Tucker Stark, conveyed the same information to me. He is a cohort of Pendergast and Hutchins, and heard it from the horse's mouth."

"I know McGraw," Talbot said, scratching his head, "and he's an honest man."

"Well, Stark's not, but he knows the truth."

Just about that time, Gunter Kauffmann coughed and rolled over to get to his feet. Sam had dropped the Winchester back in Kauffmann's room, so at first glance, none of them seemed armed. Sam shoved Kauffmann back to the ground, and jerked up his shirt, pointing to the puckered wound in his side.

"That's where Liam shot him, trying to defend himself from Kauffmann's shotgun. He hid that wound from everyone, knowing it would condemn him."

"That looks like a gunshot wound, all right," Talbot said.

Kauffmann jerked the shirttail back down, while climbing to his feet.

The big German stepped back toward the outside doorway, his eyes full of hate as he glared at both Sam and the judge.

As he backed away, Talbot cautioned him, "Don't leave here, or I'll have to send the marshal after you. I want to find out —"

Kauffmann didn't wait, but sprang back through the door. Talbot reached over to the dresser top, grabbed a small Smith and Wesson from under a face towel, and turned as if to bring it to bear on Sam, as he tried to caution him, "Don't you leave either," but before he could fully turn, Sam wrenched the weapon away from him, and headed for the outside door. He wasn't about to let Kauffmann get away now.

As he charged through the doorway, Kauffmann was already coming back out through his room's window, Sam's Winchester in hand.

He worked the lever on the Winchester as he brought it up, but again, wasn't fast enough, as Sam centered the little Smith and Wesson on Kauffmann's chest and fired. Kauffmann looked surprised, but continued to try and raise the Winchester. Sam fired again, and again, and Kauffmann stumbled back against the rail, and plunged over, his arms flailing, careening down a story into the alley behind the hotel.

The judge was making his way out the hallway door when Sam looked back inside. "Don't bother, Judge Talbot."

He stopped and looked back, his eyes flaring wide as his own Smith and Wesson came up in Sam's hand, but Sam flipped it around and caught it by the barrel, crossed the room, and handed it to the surprised judge.

"Now," Sam said with a deep sigh, "let's get this all straightened out."

"You're surrendering yourself?"

"I am, presuming that son of a bitch that shot my brother is not going anywhere."

"Where is he?" Talbot asked.

"Out in the alley, down below. He took a dive off the balcony after taking a couple of shots from that little peashooter of yours. . . ."

"You shot him down?"

"I shot him rather than have him shoot me. He had my own rifle coming down on me."

They heard footsteps pounding down the hall, and Marshal Clark Peckham ran to the doorway and charged in, his weapon quickly leveled on Sam.

"Don't be hasty, Marshal," the judge cautioned. "Mr. Stranahan here has already given himself up, wanting to get things straightened out."

"He can straighten things out all right, sittin' in my jail, or what's left of it."

"You got other items to take care of at the moment. You got a man all shot up out in the alley, or so Mr. Stranahan says, and a couple more . . . Where did you say, Stranahan?"

"They're up at Miss Maureen's Sporting House," Sam said, then added, "There's a reward out for both of them, and I want to collect it."

The hell —" Clark started to complain, but the judge stopped him short.

"Then," the judge added, "you got to go over to the Miner's Hall and tell them the trial is postponed until tomorrow. Will that give us time to get all this down in writing, Mr. Stranahan?"

"Should do just fine, Judge."

"Let's go get some breakfast and talk this over. I'm interested to hear more about Sheriff Thacker. I never did much care for the slacker."

"My pleasure. After we make sure that Kauffmann hasn't gone anywhere."

"Clark, handle that, will you, so Mr.

Stranahan has some peace of mind?"

"Humph," Peckham managed, but strode out.

"Breakfast," Sam said. "Then I owe the barber a half dollar and he owes me a shave and a tub of hot bathwater."

By late that afternoon, Gunter Kauffmann's body was alongside that of Norval Hutchins, both bound to a plank and leaned up against the barber's wall under his overhang out of the snow. Even with regular snowflakes the size of dimes drifting down, the roadway was full of observers. It seemed that Kauffmann was probably dead before he'd hit the alleyway behind the Kaiser. Three shots from the little Smith and Wesson lay within a hand span in the center of his chest.

Gordon Pendergast had had his visit with the doc, and his leg was well bandaged. It seemed that a half dozen soiled doves were prepared to testify that he had confessed to the robbery of the Bozeman stage along with Hutchins and Pacovsky, and that they had done so at the behest of Sheriff Hiram Thacker. Tucker Stark had chimed in and signed a written statement that he had heard the late Norval Hutchins brag about the crime, as well as had the man in the next cell, Gordy Pendergast.

No one was able to directly connect Gunter Kauffmann to the death of Liam Stranahan, but the wound in his side and the testimony of Maureen O'Toole that Betsylou Maddigan had identified the voice of Kauffmann hiring Stark to kill Liam Stranahan, and Kauffmann's own actions in front of the judge, seemed enough for Judge Talbot. Then when Stark backed her testimony up as well as testified that he'd seen Kauffmann with a bloody side late in the afternoon after Liam had been killed, and that Kauffmann had bragged to him that he'd killed Liam . . . well, the judge was more than satisfied.

All Stark got out of it was the promise of a beefsteak every night until he was to hang.

Later in the evening, it was a steak that Sam was treating Miss Maureen to in the dining room of the Kaiser.

Judge Horace Talbot sat across the room, placating Clark Peckham with a dozen oysters and a beefsteak, and the fact that Sam Stranahan had promised restitution by rebuilding the jail wall. The judge not only tipped his hat to Sam and Maureen, but sent them a bottle of fine champagne.

Sam enjoyed his conversation with Maureen, and they'd come to an agreement. Before he left, he dropped by the judge's table, thanked him for the champagne, and spoke to the marshal. "You've got a Remington revolver of mine."

"I'm keepin' it as evidence," the marshal said.

"Give it back to him," the judge said, his tone admonishing.

The marshal flushed, but acquiesced. "Come by the office tomorrow."

That night, Sam, in the same room Gunter Kauffmann had enjoyed, slept the sleep of the satisfied, his brother avenged, his name cleared with the law. His future plans well laid out.

When he arose, Sam rented a good saddle horse from Erik Vandermer, and led it up to Miss Maureen's Sporting House. He and Maureen spent all day riding up to the Siglinda One and Two, and back. While there, they inspected the property . . . their property. To their surprise the two Chinese laborers were hard at work on a vein that Gunter Kauffmann had shown them.

A very rich vein that began just inside the mouth of the mine.

They said it had been well hidden behind a piece of ricking, and they wondered why it hadn't been worked long before. Sam concluded that Kauffmann had discovered it, and hidden it from Liam.

Which was the reason Kauffmann had been so anxious to buy Liam out, or get rid of him any way he could.

The next morning Sam set off at a lope, enjoying a beautiful crisp, clear winter's day. He headed south, for the pass that Silas McGraw said was the McGraws' destination.

By late afternoon, he sighted a wisp of smoke coming from a behind a stand of chokecherries, and gave his heels to the grulla until he reined up beyond them, near where the McGraws were busily putting the finishing touches on a dugout in a side hill overlooking a small creek.

Mary stood on the cabin roof, laying sod, a smudge of dirt on her cheek, looking as beautiful as Sam had ever seen her . . . or any other woman.

Silas had seen him coming, and stood with his hands on his hips. When Sam reined up and leaped from the horse, Silas guffawed, then said, "Well, ol' coon, you ain't strung from no tree. I swear, you're a fairly respectable-lookin' gent, with all that fur shed."

"I'm doing just fine. Don't work too hard on that cabin, as you're going back with me in the morning."

"You need help with them owl hoots?"

"No, sir. Them owl hoots are all where they belong."

"Then jus' where you think we're a-goin'?"

We're going to my mine, and you and I are gonna get rich doing a little mud grubbing. We got a fine cabin —"

"I hate that work. I done it some back in sixty-five, an' decided I ain't no pocket gopher."

"I was up there, Silas, and you and I, and Miss Maureen, won't have to work ever again if this vein holds out and we put in a year or so of hard work."

Silas contemplated that for a while. "Don't think so, ol' coon. Mrs. McGraw and I like the clean air and the critters."

"Well, sir, in that case, we've got other business. I'm straight with the law."

"That's a right fine thing."

"So . . ."

"So?"

"So, I'd like to have a talk with you about Miss Mary."

Silas laughed and slapped his thighs, then suddenly turned serious. "Tell you what, I'll jus' hold on to them gold coins